Cane's Promise
Forever Midnight MC
Book One

Victoria Gale

Published in 2020 by

Deryn Publishing

United Kingdom

First Edition

© 2020 Deryn Publishing

All characters, places and events are fictional. Any resemblance to real persons, places or events is purely coincidental.

The moral rights of the author have been asserted.

All rights reserved. No part of this publication may be reproduced, copied, stored or distributed in any form, without prior written permission of the publisher

"Never befriend the oppressed unless you are prepared to take on the oppressor."

– Ogden Nash

PROLOGUE

I headed to the kitchen for a late-night snack. I'd skipped dinner and needed something in my stomach, otherwise I would never sleep.

Voices sounded downstairs. I froze and listened for a second before huffing out a relieved breath: Mom and Tony, my stepdad. They must be watching a late-night movie or something. I tiptoed down the stairs and across the hall, and then opened the kitchen door, being careful to close it as quietly as possible. Even so, I winced when the inevitable click sounded.

With no artificial light coming from either inside or outside the house, I used only the moonlight streaming through the window and patio doors to guide my way. I edged around the center island and rushed to the fridge, but as I opened the door, something made the hair on my neck stand up.

My heart pounded. Someone was in the room with me.

I couldn't say how I knew. There was no noise or sense of movement. Just years of experience.

"I missed you at dinner, Thea."

Hearing Daniel's voice made my breaths come in shallow, panicked gasps. I'd been stupid to come, but Mom had said he had business in town this evening. I wanted to flee, to hide, but my feet felt as though they'd been nailed to the floor and moving would cause them unfathomable damage and pain.

It took every ounce of strength I had, but after a moment, I reached into the fridge and pulled out an apple before closing it and turning to face the direction his voice had come from.

He emerged from the shadows surrounding the patio doors. Silver moonlight reflected on his dark slicked-back hair and highlighted his sharp, angular face. As usual, he wore an expensive suit, also dark. He'd loosened the tie from his neck and unbuttoned the collar of his shirt. A whiskey glass rested half-empty in his hand. With a sneer on his face, he looked every inch the psychopathic bastard he was.

I looked from him to the entrance leading to the hall. If I ran flat out, would I make it to my bedroom where I could lock the door, or better yet, my car?

"I said, I missed you at dinner," he repeated before taking a sip from his glass. "It shows good manners to respond when someone engages you in conversation. Do you need a session to teach you good manners?"

"No, Daniel," I said far too quickly. I lifted my chin and

clenched my apple as tight as I could in an attempt to keep my hands from shaking. "Please pardon my rudeness. I was just surprised by your presence. If you'll excuse me, it's late and I'm very tired."

I edged toward the door. Daniel did too. He reached it before me.

"I haven't seen you in a while." He brushed a strand of hair from my face and pushed it behind my ear. I stiffened. "Anyone would think you're avoiding me. Missing dinners, making sure you're out when I'm around." He glanced down at my body. "Covering up."

Despite the summer heat, I'd decked myself in a set of thick flannel pajamas and topped those with a full-length dressing gown tightly drawn. I could hardly breathe, but it was worth it to keep his eyes off me.

Daniel smiled at my obvious discomfort.

"I missed you on your birthday. Did you get my present?"

"Yes." The red lingerie set went straight in the bin.

"Yes, what?"

"Yes, Daniel."

"And what else do have to you say?"

For the first time, I turned my head toward him, but kept my gaze no higher than his nose. "Thank you, Daniel."

"It's a shame you only show manners when prompted. I'd

blame your upbringing, but..." He shrugged and was about to say more when the door swung open. Daniel stepped out of view behind it, but I stood face to face with Mom.

She glanced at my nightwear and the apple in my hand and tsked. "I might have known I'd find you scrounging for food. If you'd eaten the dinner, I spent over an hour preparing, you wouldn't have to."

"I wasn't hungry," I said and looked at my feet. Conscious that Daniel stood behind me, I added, "I'm sorry."

"Hmm. You should be. There are leftovers in the fridge. Heat them so all my hard work doesn't go completely to waste." She slurred her words, and I could see from the white specks lining her nostrils that she'd been doing more than drinking. She placed her hands on my hips. "Besides," she said, "you don't want to get too skinny and lose all your lovely curves. Not that anyone can see them beneath that get-up. You couldn't look less feminine if you tried."

With that, she pushed me to the side and tottered over to the fridge, muttering something about my wasting the figure her good genes had blessed me with.

"I should go. Goodnight, Mom."

She turned. "No, no, no, young lady. I said you should eat and you're going to."

Daniel stepped out from behind the door. I flinched when he

placed a hand on my shoulder.

"Mom's right," he said. "We wouldn't want you to lose those lovely curves."

"Ah, Dan. I didn't realize you were still here. Can I get you a drink?"

"I have one, thank you." He lifted his glass and waved it at Mom.

"So, you do. Then let me offer you a top-up, and I'll grab another for your father and myself while I'm at it."

He waved away her offer. "I shouldn't. It's late and I have an early morning."

"Of course." She tilted her head at me and continued, "A conversation with this one is enough to put anyone to sleep."

"Not at all. Thea's been great company. We were just discussing her lack of proper manners, but there's no need to worry; I'm certain the next time we meet, she'll show me the appropriate level of gratitude required for the thought I put into her birthday present."

Mom stared at me for a moment. I couldn't quite read the look on her face. She knew what Daniel's present had been, but rather than being furious that my stepbrother had chosen such an inappropriate gift, she marveled at the quality of the silk and the expense he must have gone to.

Her eyes wandered to Daniel's hand still resting on my

shoulder. I wanted to smack it away and scream in his face, demand he never came near me again, but self-preservation stilled my hand.

One day… one day, he'd pay. He'd meet someone he couldn't push around, and they'd end him. My soul screamed, wishing that person was me.

Mom turned and pulled a bottle of red wine from the cupboard. She set it on the counter and gathered glasses.

Daniel trailed his hand down my back. Nausea churned my stomach, and I pushed back the bile rising in my throat. He pressed his mouth close to my ear. "I retrieved your gift and placed it in your top drawer. Next time I see you, I expect you to be wearing it." He pulled back and downed his glass before handing it to me. "And I meant what I said. I'll expect you to show an appropriate level of gratitude, as well as make recompense for your callous disregard for the trouble I went to. Perhaps a session will be required after all."

He moved back to the patio doors, bade goodnight to Mom and left. I stood frozen for a moment, too afraid to move or speak, praying that he'd gone, and I'd never see him again. But that was nothing more than a fruitless wish I'd made countless times.

My muscles quivered and I tried to release the tension in my body. I stared at Mom as she opened the bottle and poured two glasses. When a light came on in the converted pool-house where Daniel lived, I released the breath I'd been holding.

"How could you stand there and do nothing?" My pulse pounded in my ears as my pent-up anger and frustration built. I rushed to the center island and slammed his glass on the countertop, half wishing it would smash. "How could you have brought me to this hell hole?"

Her lips thinned and curled on one side. "Tony and Dan work hard every day to keep a roof over our heads and put food on the table—"

"Tony's a lowlife drug dealer who lets his men do all his dirty work for him, and Dan's a sick fuck who should be ended so he can't hurt anyone." I didn't need to add that she was the brains behind their whole operation. She knew.

Her hand shook as she reached for her wine glass and took a swig. Some of the dark red liquid dribbled down the side of the glass. She licked it off, before placing the glass back on the countertop.

"You ungrateful little bitch." A smile played on her lips as she stared at me. "You're twenty-one and not a child anymore. It's about time you learned your duty to this family. Dan's a little unusual in his desires." She chuckled. "Hell, he's wanted you for years. If that doesn't show how twisted he is, then nothing does."

"Daniel's more than twisted, he's… he's… a sadist and a perv."

"See, that's where you need to grow up. All men are pervs. It's about time you gave him what he wanted, earned your keep. The only reason Tony instructed him to keep away for so long was because of your age. You're a grown woman now. There's no need for him to keep waiting."

"Other than the fact that I hate the thought of being in the same room as him, and, oh, he happens to be my brother."

"Stepbrother. It's not as though you have the same blood and were brought up together. He was eighteen when I married his father. Nine years is long enough." She reached out and placed her manicured hand on my cheek. "Stop being a cock tease."

"Cock tease?" I batted her hand away. "What happened to you? When did you become this person? Before Dad died—"

"You know nothing of my life before your father died. You were just a child at the time."

"I know we were happy. You were happy. Not some vindictive cow who treats people like commodities."

"I've worked hard to give you the best life I could, but always, always this ungrateful backtalk. Dan was right about your lack of manners. We should have let him have more sessions with you over the years. Maybe then you'd have a better understanding of what's what."

My insides rolled at the thought of going down to the basement with Daniel. I knew what was what. I'd seen the shift in his eyes when his desire to hurt and control me had developed into something sexual.

Oblivious to my discomfort or ignoring it, Mom waved her hand around to encompass the whole of our mansion kitchen. This one room was twice the size of the apartment we'd lived in with Dad, and more than twice as expensive to run. "It's time you realized that without Tony and Dan, we'd likely be crack whores somewhere doing whatever we could to make ends meet."

I scoffed and shook my head. "It's funny that you think you're not a crack whore."

The words were no sooner out of my mouth when Mom pulled her hand back and slapped me across the face. As soon as she drew away, she lifted the wine bottle with her shaking hand and pressed it to her lips, barely taking a breath as she swigged almost the whole thing.

Tears leaked from my eyes and my cheek felt as though it was on fire. Normally I'd put ice on it, but right then, I wanted nothing more than to be out of the kitchen… out of the house. Forever.

I pushed away from the counter. "I'm going to bed. Goodnight. Mother."

"He's very attractive, you know," she called after me. "His body could have been sculpted by the Gods, and those abs… If I were twenty years younger, I'd take a shot at him myself."

Bile rose in my throat, but I turned to face her. "You're welcome to him," I said.

She raised the bottle as though toasting something with me. "Oh, darling, you're not as precious as you think you are. Remember that. Just open those tightly sealed legs and give us all some peace. Who knows, you might even learn to enjoy Dan's little… quirks."

Without another word, I left the kitchen and ran up the stairs. Mom followed behind me. "There's no use running away," she said. "You know how well that goes. It's better to accept your fate."

I rushed into the bedroom, but even in my agitated state and with Daniel in the pool house, I knew better than to slam the door. Instead, I gently closed it and slid the bolts I'd screwed into place before sagging to the floor.

I shut my eyes tighter than I'd shut the door, wanting for all the world to be somewhere else, anywhere else. Silent tears streamed down my face. Mom was right. I did know how well my attempts at running away had gone before. We both did, but things would be different this time. This time, I'd made a proper plan.

CHAPTER ONE

(Two Months Later)

Cane

"Well, ain't the lot of you a sight for sore eyes," Cherrie said while placing her hands on her hips.

I ran my hand over my beard and wondered if it could do with cutting back and inch or two. Hell, the brotherhood had been on the road for so long, my hair had gotten a bit out of hand and needed tying back to save it from blasting into my face on the bike.

"Your ass is looking fine as always," Lucky said before Cherrie whipped at him with the cloth she always carried around to wipe down surfaces.

"You say that like I ain't old enough to be your old Ma."

Lucky laughed. "I'll be sure to tell my Ma you think she's old next time I see her."

I smiled at their banter before reaching out to pull Cherrie in for a hug. Each of my brothers repeated the action with Lucky being sure to add a quick slap to her backside soon after.

"And you'll be wanting me to tell Greg how you're manhandling his woman," Cherrie said with a devilish grin on her face.

Lucky pulled out a chair at the table and sat down. "We'll just call it quits," he said. "You don't tell Greg and I won't tell Ma."

"And Lucky pulls off another lucky escape," Bono said. He was Lucky alright, lucky Cherrie had a soft spot for him and let him get away with that shit.

Everyone laughed while I took my seat at the head of the table. "What's going on, Cherrie?" I asked as soon as they'd sobered. "Caleb said you had a problem."

We'd been touring the territory, checking on businesses the brothers owned from town to town, reading the local mood, dealing with any problems with the local gangs, and fucking the local women. A trip my brothers and I sure found a lot of fun making. We'd left our home base and Midnight Anchor not two months back and hadn't expected to return for another three weeks.

When my brother, Caleb, President of the Forever Midnight Motorcycle Club called saying he had his hands full with the Feral Sons, we weren't expecting to be sent on a detour to

Midnight Anchor, but here we were.

"Well, it's hard to explain really," she said. "And probably nothing."

Lucky sat back in his chair and shook his head. "You ain't gonna be calling Caleb for nothing," he said. "Now, what's the problem? You and Greg having any trouble?"

He might play around with Cherrie from time to time, but when it came right down to it, he loved her like she was his own Ma. We all did.

"Not on your life. Not anyone around here gonna mess with us. The brothers may be busy with those damn Feral Sons, but they'd be here in an instant if there was any real trouble."

She was damn right about that. Greg was a member of our family. Cherrie too. Even if you grew old, settled down and didn't ride out with us that often, once you're a brother of Forever Midnight, you're always a brother, and we take care of our own. Not that the two of them would need our help.

Cherrie sighed before pulling the only spare chair remaining out from the table and sitting down. "Well," she said. "Just a week or so after you left, we had a visitor here at the bar."

Lucky sat forward and clenched his fists. "This visitor the source of your trouble?"

"Cool your engine. She's a slip of a thing and no bother to you." Cherrie raised a hand and glanced at the door behind her.

"She here now?" I asked.

"She is. Tony and I put her up in the spare room upstairs. She's been working and earning her keep."

I leaned forward and placed my arms on the table. No-one said anything for a moment, but Cherrie sat firm under my gaze.

"You in the habit of taking in fucking strays now?" I asked, wondering what the hell we were doing. No wonder Caleb hadn't come to look at this himself. We had enough shit of our own to deal with without needing to take on some bitch's abusive ex or pimp. "What kind of shit is this girl dragging?"

Cherrie fluffed her hair and glared back at me. She and Greg may be in their sixties and happy to run the bar now, but back in the day, Greg was my Dad's second in command. He was a badass fucker when he needed to be, and Cherrie as his old woman had some standing. You might even say she was Queen Bitch after my Mom left. Hell, I'd seen her shoot some stupid fucker in the balls for grabbing her pussy. They'd mellowed with age, but that didn't mean they were to be messed with. That's why it was so strange for her to be taking in some stupid ho.

"Jess ain't your usual stray," she said. "She's a good girl, well-spoken."

"Not someone who belongs here," I said, trying to read between the lines.

Cherrie smiled and glanced at Jameson.

He gave her a nod and cleared his throat. He was a man of few words, but when he spoke, everyone listened. "All people belong in the place they choose to make their home," he said.

"Fucking right," Lucky added.

Jameson hadn't had the same upbringing as the rest of my brothers. He'd been privately educated, went to college even, but he belonged with our family. Although, seeing him walk into the bar all those years ago with his fancy suit and polished shoes, you'd be hard-pressed to think that would ever be so.

"So, what's the girl's story?" Rex asked, speaking for the first time.

"Not a clue. She's a runaway, I know that much. But she's as tight-lipped as a nun vowed to silence, as innocent too, so don't none of you go treating her like no dolly girl. You especially, not a finger on her, you hear?" she said pointing at Lucky. "I see how she reacts every time one of those reprobates we call customers pats her behind. She's as jittery as a cat on a hot tin roof. No raising your voice none, neither."

It was a big ask. If there was anything my brothers liked as much as riding their bikes and a good punch up, it was fucking women, and every single one was fair game until they said otherwise. Hell, they'd take any bitch as long as she had a working pussy and wasn't already claimed by a brother. Though from the little Cherrie had said, this Jess sure didn't sound like the type of woman we were used to meeting.

Lucky placed his hand on his heart. "Not an unwanted finger. Not a loudly spoken word. On my honor," he said seriously before adding a cheeky smile. "But if she throws herself at me, a man's gotta do what a man's gotta do."

"That's good enough for me," Cherrie said, as each brother said the same.

"How exactly do you think we can help her?" I asked. If the girl had been here for over a month and Cherrie hadn't managed to pull her story out of her, then I sure as hell didn't how we'd pull it off.

"I haven't got a clue," she said. "Hell, every day I'm surprised she's still around and hasn't fled to the wind already. I've been wishing you boys would get here before that happened. Since you've pulled off that minor miracle, you can sure as hell figure out what to do next."

"Fine," I said, resolved to do my damnedest. No matter how much of a fucking waste of time I thought it was. I may not know this girl from Adam, but she wasn't the one asking, Cherrie was, and for her, I'd lay down my life. "We'd better meet her first."

Cherrie smiled and stood from the table. "I'll send her in to take your order so you can get a read on her. Take it easy and don't push for nothing. We'll play it by ear."

"Yes, Ma," Lucky said and saluted, earning him another cuff

with her cloth.

CHAPTER TWO

Thea

"**H**ey, Sweet-cheeks. Another whiskey for the road."

I stiffened for a second before swatting the hand away from my bottom. Resisting the urge to growl and scream for him never to touch me again, I collected the empty glass from the table.

It was the same thing every day: horny regulars and drunks who thought that because I worked in the bar, I was public property. For the most part, I'd found them to be harmless, but a well of dread always sank in the pit of my stomach at the slightest male touch or raised voice.

"No more for you, Frank," I said, knowing Frank was a patron who simply got a bit handsy when he'd had a glass or two. "Hand over your keys and I'll get Greg to call you a cab home." Frank reluctantly delved into his pocket and placed the keys in my hand, while I was careful not to shy away from the gesture.

I often considered finding a better place to work, one where the clientele wasn't so rough around the edges, but I knew appearances were deceiving. Just because someone was smartly attired on the outside, it didn't mean they had a warm and caring heart.

No, Midnight Anchor was the best place for me to be. Somewhere Daniel would never think to look. It was easy to handle the occasional pawing when I knew what was at stake if my family found me.

At least for now.

Though a part of me knew I'd taken too big a risk and stayed in one place too long already.

I sighed and glanced across the room to the bar. Greg polished a Pilsner glass with his cloth and set it on the shelf. He might look intimidating with his muscles the size of tires, and the tattoos covering his arms, but if I hadn't met him and his wife, Cherrie, I didn't know what I'd have done. They'd taken me in like a lost puppy and given me a job. No questions asked. As I said, looks can be deceiving. Although over the last month or so, I'd confided in Cherrie that I'd run away from home, I hadn't had the strength to tell her the reason why, but I thought she'd understand the day I didn't turn up for work and all my things were gone from the room they let me use upstairs.

"Jess, I could use a favor," Cherrie said as I walked back

towards the bar. She fluffed her powder-puff pink hair and gave me a wink. "I need to use the little girls' room. The owners are set up in the back room. See if they need anything, will you?"

A flicker of confusion rushed through my mind as I'd believed Greg and Cherrie the owners of the bar and hadn't met anyone else who seemed to fill that role in all the time I'd been working there.

Cherrie was about to rush away, but quickly turned back. "They can come across a little... intimidating," she said. "But don't be fooled, they're a bunch of softies at heart. At least to family. I'll be there to help you in a short while."

With that, and without giving me a chance to respond, Cherrie darted off in the direction of the restroom.

"I guess, I'll go serve the owners in the back room," I said to thin air as a weight settled on my shoulders. If the owners weren't happy with my employment, I'd be back on the road sooner than anticipated.

I shoved Frank's keys into my pocket and pushed my way through the crowds to the back door marked private, and hesitated while attempting to still the sense of dread building inside me. I pictured a group of men dressed in business suits, all drinking whiskey. I glanced once more at Greg behind the bar. He caught my gaze, smiled and nodded before proceeding to serve the customer before him.

I took a deep breath and steadied my irrational nerves. If Cherrie thought the bosses had hearts of gold, then they must have. She wouldn't send me in there alone otherwise.

I knocked on the door and waited a while for a response before daring to enter. When none came, I twisted the door handle and stepped inside.

Four men sat around the table, another stood at its head. Five very intense, very scary-looking sets of eyes turned in my direction. My eyes locked on the man standing and my breath stilled. If Greg's muscles were the size of tires, this guy's were the size of monster-truck tires. Tattoos didn't just cover his arms, they reached out from the top of his black T-shirt and traveled up his neck towards his beard. His hair was dark with blond highlights, and pulled back, making me think it must be long. Everything about him was terrifying, yet captivating.

Worried that I was staring, I pulled my gaze from his face, but the tight T-shirt visible beneath his black leather jacket hugged every muscle like a second skin and drew my attention to the smoking hot body beneath. I found myself staring again.

He looked as though he was about to say something when the words, 'Cherrie sent me,' escaped from my lips. "C-can I get you anything?"

"I'll have a beer," one of the men sat at the table said.

For the first time, I turned my attention to them. They

were massive, although not as large or commanding as the man standing. Each wore the same leather jacket, and I noted that it had some kind of skull logo on the back. Greg had the same jacket, as did lots of the other bikers who frequented the bar, but I'd never seen these particular men before.

"Beer here too," another one said.

"Let's make it easy on the girl and all have beer, shall we, brothers?" the man standing said in a low voice that sent shivers down my spine.

My eyes darted to him, and he gave me a slight frown. Even so, I couldn't help but imagine my hands caressing his chest and the six-pack I was certain lay beneath his clothing.

Embarrassed by my reaction to him, I mumbled an affirmation and rushed from the room as quickly as I could, headed for the bar.

"Five beers, please?" I said to Greg as soon as he was within hearing distance. Although I couldn't for the life of me fathom why I was in such a rush to get back.

"Any particular kind?" he asked.

I looked down at my feet as a flush crept over my cheeks. "I'm sorry," I said. "I didn't check."

"Hell, no worries. We'll give them something generic. If they complain, we'll tell them to be more specific in the future."

"Thank you. I am truly sorry."

He froze for a moment and shook his head while giving me a funny look. "It's really not that big a deal." Greg reached for a glass and was about to draft a beer when he looked at me again. "Actually, you were headed into the back room, if memory serves me right."

"That's right," I said.

"Then I know just the beer they want," he said, giving me a wink.

A wave of relief washed over me as I remembered Cherrie saying that the men inside were the owners. Greg knew their preferences. I really wasn't keen on heading back to them and telling them they could like their beer or lump it.

He put the glass down and grabbed five bottles from the fridge before popping the tops off them and placing them on the counter. "You manage that lot without a tray?" he asked while glancing around to see if he could spot one.

"I'll be fine, thank you," I said and smiled. Cherrie had taught me how to hook three bottles between the fingers of each hand.

Greg shook his head at me again. "Always with the please and thank yous. You sure been brought up with some fine manners."

I stiffened at his words and almost dropped the bottle I'd just picked up. Greg noticed and reached out a hand towards me. I flinched back and Greg withdrew and scowled at me as though

I'd slapped him across the face.

"I-I'd better get these back to the room." I snatched up the bottles and practically ran across the bar floor.

So stupid! Greg had only been making a casual observation, but my mind flashed back to the last time I'd seen Daniel. If he ever caught me, that promised session on manners would be a million times worse than anything I'd experienced before.

I sighed and cast a quick look back. For the third time that shift, I thought about leaving. Maybe, the time had come for me to move on.

I composed myself at the door, but looking down at the handle, I realized with all the bottles in my hands I couldn't open it. I shifted the beer around, managing a fourth in one hand and two under the crook of my elbow, and turned the knob, using my foot to inch the door open. With a quick shift around, I returned the bottles to their original location and entered the room.

Once again, all eyes turned to me, but this time they all came from people sitting down. I avoided their gaze and looked at the floor, moving around the table and putting one beer in front of each person.

I hesitated in front of the big guy. His sweet honey scent, overlaid with dirt and engine oil, cut through the stench of beer and smoke that permeated the club. As I placed his bottle on the table, the guy to his left reached out and grabbed my wrist.

Before I had the chance to react, the big guy stood from his chair and growled, "Get your fucking hands off her, Rex."

I'd never heard a voice so angry and wanted nothing more than to run. Rex must have felt the same way as he released me without a moment's hesitation and raised his hands in supplication. Clutching the remaining two bottles to my chest, I backed into the corner and stared at the floor, unsure what else to do.

"Cane," Rex said. "You need to check her necklace." A tension hung over the room, but Rex continued. "I've seen its like before. It's a fucking tracker."

I dropped the bottles, vaguely registering Cane's voice demanding to know who I worked for. They shattered and sent a spray of glass and liquid over my legs. My hand flew to the black-heart pendant at my neck.

A tracker? No. It can't be. It can't be.

My whole body shook. I was going to be sick. Mom had given me this gift as a sixteenth birthday present. I only ever took it off in the shower and at bedtime.

Every time… every time I'd run away, they knew where to find me. But… but why was now different?

I dropped to the floor.

This time wasn't different. Daniel knew. Daniel knew, and he was playing with me. This was a lesson to be learned. No matter how far I ran, no matter how long I was free, he would come for me.

My hands shook uncontrollably, but I had to get the necklace from off my neck. I tugged and tugged at the chain. It was strong. I'd always thought it thicker than necessary for the pendant it held, but now realized that was to make it hard to break. It cut into my neck, but I had to get it off and I couldn't manage the clasp. Not now.

Someone grabbed hold of my hands and stopped them from pulling on the chain. A deep soothing voice reached my ears, but my thoughts drowned out his words. I looked up and saw Cane's deep brown eyes filled with concern. His mouth was moving, but I still couldn't hear his voice.

"Get it off," I muttered.

There was a slight commotion to my right. I shifted my gaze and saw Cherrie enter the room. At her presence, all sound returned to my ears.

"What the fuck is going on?" she demanded and charged over, barreling Cane out the way. Everyone glanced from her to Cane. I could tell it wasn't usual for someone to talk to him that way, but at that moment, I couldn't care what that meant. I registered a brief loss as his hands left mine, but Cherrie's face filled my vision.

"What happened, sweetie?" she asked and touched a finger

to my neck. She pulled it away with blood on the tip.

"Get it off," I said again before screaming the words. I clawed at the chain again, but no matter how hard I tugged, it wouldn't come off.

This time, Cherrie was the one who grabbed my hands. "I'll get it off. Just stay still, you're hurting yourself." I gave a brief nod to show I understood, and Cherrie reached around my neck and undid the clasp. She tossed it to Cane and turned to face me, wiping the tears running down my cheeks. "There, it's gone, okay? It's gone."

I looked into her concerned eyes and shook my head. "It doesn't matter," I said after a moment. "He knows where I am. He's always known. He'll come for me."

"Not if I have anything to fucking say about it." Cane's voice rang with a resolve I'd never heard before. It resonated through my whole body and made me feel that maybe, just for a second, everything would be okay.

He slammed the pendant on the table and ground it beneath the base of his beer bottle. After it broke into pieces, he lifted what looked like a SIM card from inside the remains. All hope fled from me.

Daniel knew where I was. Daniel would come and get me.

I lifted my knees and clenched them to my chest, burying my head as tightly as I could against them. Cherrie stroked my hair. From her breathing, I wondered if she might be talking, but once again, my ability to hear the words and comprehend what she was saying had left me.

CHAPTER THREE

Cane

"Shit, we smell worse than a decomposing body," Jameson said, lamenting our lack of personal hygiene.

Lucky sniffed his pit. "Speak for yourself," he said. "I smell like a bed of roses."

I cuffed him over his head. "You fucking stink worse than the rest of us."

We all smelled like motor oil, sweat, and the road, but not one of us wanted to keep Cherrie waiting longer than necessary. We had come to the bar as soon as we'd arrived in town. I was about to cuff Lucky over the head for being a smart-ass when a knock sounded at the door.

Silence fell over the room, and we waited for something to happen. Jameson looked at me and raised an eyebrow. We weren't used to someone knocking before entering a room. When no one appeared, I was about to shout for them to come in already, but remembered our oath to Cherrie: *'not a loudly spoken word'*. I shook my head and stood to answer the door.

It opened before I had the chance to take a single step.

Fuck!

The woman before me was not what I expected. Cherrie called her a girl, because of that, and her being a runaway, I'd pictured a minor, but this woman… fuck… This woman was all woman. She was beautiful. I flicked my gaze down her tall, slender body. Long brown hair hung in a braid over one shoulder. Despite her height, she seemed fragile and small. The baggy T-shirt she wore over loose-fitting jeans looked like some expensive shit that came from a high-end boutique and did little to conceal the curves beneath. Most remarkable of all, were the big green eyes that popped out of her head, making her look like a motherfucking doe caught in the headlights.

All people may belong in the place they choose to make their home, but this woman screamed innocence and purity. She also screamed money, like some fucking debutante on her way to a ball. Even if she was trying to hide the fact. She sure as hell didn't belong in a bar like Midnight Anchor, and she certainly didn't belong in a room with the likes of us.

But fuck! Every time her eyes landed on me, the thought of licking from her goddamn nipples to her pussy surfaced in my mind.

I opened my mouth to say something, though damned if I knew what, when she squeaked some barely audible words.

Only when Jameson ordered a beer did I register that she'd asked if she could get us anything. It took Bono to order another for me to come to my senses and suggest we all have the same.

I couldn't get thoughts of her and what I'd like to do to her out of my mind. We'd sworn not to lay a finger on her. A brief moment of weakness told me my cock sure as hell wasn't my finger. No one said anything about that, but I shrugged the thought away. It was the spirit of the promise that counted, not the words. Although, if she threw herself at me, that would be a different matter. Damn, I hoped the look she gave me when she entered meant she'd do just that.

It felt like forever before she returned. This time there was no knock, but she fumbled at the door, and it opened just a crack for a few seconds before she entered. I couldn't get my eyes off her delicate face as she walked around the table, placing a beer in front of each of my brothers. Her gaze never left the floor, but she hesitated for a moment when she put mine down. Fuck, she was so close I could feel her body heat, and practically taste her scent of milk and sunshine in the air.

Before I knew what was happening, Rex snatched out his hand and grabbed her by the wrist. A burning rage built inside me. Not only had he broken his promise to Cherrie, but he'd also placed his hand on a woman I'd already decided was mine.

The events that happened in the next few minutes were a bundle of confusion. I wanted to rip Rex's fucking head from his shoulders and shove it up his ass. But as soon as he'd told me the girl wore a tracker, that rage shifted to her. Rational thought left my head and worry for the brotherhood kicked in. She'd been sent to spy on us and follow our movements. No wonder she was jittery. She was shit-scared of getting caught.

A roar of accusations left my lips, but when I turned to face her, I knew I was wrong. This woman was more than jittery. She was a shattered mess, just like the bottles of beer she dropped at her feet.

All color left her face, and sweat slicked her skin. I'd never have thought it possible, but her eyes got wider. She slid down the wall to the floor and clawed at the tracker's chain. We stood frozen to the spot, but the sight of it cutting into her neck and drawing blood kicked me into action.

"Jameson, get Cherrie," I said as I rushed towards the girl and, despite my promise not to lay a finger on her, grabbed her hands to stop her from doing any more damage.

"It's alright, sweetheart," I said. "We're not going to hurt you. I need you to stop doing that, okay? Cherrie's coming."

My hands completely enveloped her slight ones. Even though I held them still, they trembled within my grip.

Shit! Cherrie had asked us to take it easy on the girl, and we'd fucking broken her.

And I'd practically turned into a motherfucking pussy. All protective and shit over some fucked-up bitch. But when she raised those eyes to look at me and I saw the innocence and pain behind them, that protective instinct locked forever into place. I knew I'd do anything to keep her safe and make the bad things go away. She couldn't be, what... twenty, twenty-one? But those eyes carried more than a lifetime of hurt.

"Get it off," she muttered, and I wanted to rip the motherfucking tracker from her neck myself.

I could have kissed Cherrie when she barreled into the room and took control. Although when the girl's anguished scream to get it off came, the need to wrap her in my arms and keep her safe forever was overwhelming. Only Cherrie tossing the god damn tracker to me stopped me from doing just that.

I ground it beneath my bottle until it fell apart, and I spotted the SIM card within. I'd half hoped Rex had been wrong and the thing wasn't a tracker. At least that might have given the girl a little relief.

I lifted the SIM card to be sure and instantly regretted doing so.

"He knows where I am. He's always known. He'll come for me," the girl said in a hollow voice.

"Not if I have anything to fucking say about it."

Even before the words left my lips, I knew I was gonna find this fucker and rip his motherfucking head off. A promise that seared into my soul as the girl pulled herself into a tight huddle and buried her head in her knees.

Cherrie comforted her. There was no sound, but there was no mistaking that she was crying.

"I wish you hadn't done that," Rex said as he sifted through the remains of the tracker. "Ah, here it is. I might have something at home that can check the charge on this." He rushed to the door, but I yanked him back. "It's like your phone," he explained, holding up a tiny battery. "It's got a charge of a day or two tops."

I glanced at the bundled girl in the corner, wrapped in Cherrie's arms. There was no fucking way she'd been charging it. If the battery life was non-existent, I might have a glimmer of good news to share with her after all.

I released Rex and told him to call as soon as he knew anything and told Jameson to update Greg on what was going on. He was probably wondering where both Cherrie and the girl were by now.

"I'll go with him," Lucky said. "See if he's seen any strangers around lately." He glanced at the girl and back at me. "Besides, I think the fewer people crowding around her the better."

I clapped him on the shoulder to show my appreciation for his thoughtfulness, and they both left the room, leaving me alone with Cherrie and the girl.

I walked over and crouched on the floor beside them. Cherrie gave me a look that was half blame and half pleading.

"Hey, sweetheart. It's just me, you, and Cherrie here now, okay? Nobody's gonna hurt you."

Cherrie rubbed her back. "Jess. This is Cane. We're going to help you if we can, but we need to know what's going on." When she didn't answer or move a muscle besides the involuntary shaking of her body, Cherrie turned to me and said, "I'm not even sure she can hear us. What the hell happened?"

"I'll be damned if I know. Rex recognized that heart pendant as a fucking tracker. As soon as he said as much, she had a mental breakdown or something. Rex has gone to check its battery life. The fucking thing might not even be charged."

A slight shifting of movement drew both our gazes back to the girl, and she lifted her head again.

"Hey," I said, glad to see a little color returning to her cheeks. "Jess, is that your real name?"

She shook her head and glanced at Cherrie as though she were ashamed to have lied.

"Oh, honey," Cherrie said, wiping the tears from her face. "It's okay. You don't have to tell us your real name if you don't want to, but we do want to help, so if you can tell us what happened and who you're afraid of, we'll be better able to do so."

The girl's eyes darted from Cherrie to me and back again. When she spoke, her voice came out a croak. "Thea," she said. "My real name is Thea."

CHAPTER FOUR

Thea

Daniel knew where I was. He was coming for me.

Cherrie sat beside me, telling me everything would be fine, but what did she know? Greg was a good man. She'd never met Daniel, never spent a session in the basement clamped to a chair, her mouth filled with dirty rags and taped over, along with her nose. She'd never had tears streaming down her face, trying desperately to move, to break free. Not knowing if this was the time he was going to let her die.

Then Cane came. His voice tried to break into my thoughts. It felt strange, but knowing he was near made things a little better. I didn't know the first thing about him, but I did know, he was everything Daniel was not, and his presence made me feel something I hadn't felt in a long time… safe.

"… the fucking thing might not even be charged," he said, and I wanted to scoff.

It was charged.

I thought I'd made a solid plan. I'd thrown away my phone, changed cars, traveled on buses and trains, went to places they would never think to look. Used a fake name. I traveled thousands of miles, but circled back to around two-hundred-miles from home, just to throw them off track.

Daniel planned better.

A stupid sixteenth birthday present from my Mom. She told me it was a locket, sealed tight. She said she'd found an old brush Dad had used and a tiny sample of his hair alongside it. I was to never try and open it in case the hair blew away and was lost forever. I'd believed her, cherished the gift. The one and only thing I kept with me always.

I should have known better. She never loved me. All she cared about was keeping her fancy house. That meant keeping Tony happy and by extension, Daniel. No matter the cost to me.

When Cane asked if Jess was my real name, a wave of guilt washed over me. Cherrie and Greg had taken me in when they had no reason to. They'd done everything they could to help me, and how had I repaid them? By lying. It didn't matter that she said it was okay. After all the trouble I caused, I owed them that much at least.

"Thea," I said. "My real name is Thea."

Speaking came hard, as though I had to push through an

invisible barrier to be heard, and my thoughts seemed slow. All I could think was that Daniel was coming and I had to get out of here as soon as I could, but Cherrie would try to stop me.

Cane crouched so close that I felt his hot breath like fire on my skin when he spoke. But I wasn't afraid. Not of him. He reached his hand forward, but hesitated. This made me want him to touch me even more.

"I'm sorry," I said. "I never meant to cause you any trouble."

The look in his eyes when he said, "It's no trouble at all," nearly broke my heart. No-one had ever looked at me with such love and kindness before.

I suddenly became aware of the beer soaking through my jeans and onto my skin, and the shards of glass we were all sitting amongst. "We need to stand," I said before standing. The others followed.

Cane was a head taller than me and easily twice my weight. His solid presence struck deep in the center of my core, and I couldn't keep my eyes off him. Daniel could never get past such a man.

Who am I kidding? Daniel could do anything.

"We're gonna need to get you cleaned up," Cherrie said, glancing toward the door. "You think you're up for a walk through the bar?"

I straightened my spine, lifted my chin high, and walked to

the door. "I'm fine," I said before opening it. The only thing that mattered was getting away from here as quickly as I could.

Cherrie and Cane escorted me through the bar area and toward the back stairs. Whenever one of the customers came within ten feet of us, Cane would glare at them or tell them to get the F out of the way.

Heart pounding, I stopped at the door to the stairs and turned to face them. "I'll be fine by myself." I pointed to the crowded bar. "Greg could use another pair of hands and well…" my eyes lifted to Cane. "I'd rather not have you with me when I change," I said despite the fact the thought of being away from him made me feel as though my insides would shrivel up.

"If you're sure," Cherrie said.

"I'll be right here," Cane added. Muscles corded in his neck as though he was tensing for a fight. His eyes bored into me, and I feared, even after I shut the door, he'd see my actions.

His phone rang, and I tried not to huff out a breath of relief at the distraction. With a quick smile in his direction that I hoped was reassuring, I opened the door and closed it quietly behind me.

I took the first four steps at a snail's pace, worried that someone might try to follow, but when it became evident they wouldn't, I raced up the remaining steps to my room. Gathering nothing but the stash of money hidden in my drawer, I left the room and traveled to the far end of the hall where a fire escape offered a way down to the parking lot at the back of the bar. I hadn't bothered collecting my car keys as Frank's still rested in my pocket.

I yanked the window open and stepped outside into the night air. A cool wind blew strands of hair loose from my braid and whipped them around my face. I shivered and regretted my decision to not even grab a jacket. But there was no going back now.

I raced down the fire escape and into the parking lot. There were few lights on the surrounding buildings and in the alleyways, and no windows overlooked the lot. Menacing shadows filled every space amongst the silent cars. Noise filtered outside from the bar, but not a person was in sight. The back of the club left me secluded, vulnerable. I steadied my breathing. A large group of motorcycles sat idle by the far wall, and I guessed some of them must belong to Cane and the other guys. The thought of Cane brought an image of him to mind, and I froze for a second wondering if I was making the right choice; if he could really keep me safe. Wondering if I cared or if I just wanted to be near him again.

I took a deep breath and closed my eyes, allowing the gentle kiss of the night air to order my thoughts. No-one could protect me. The only thing I could do was get away from Midnight

Anchor and this town as quickly as possible. I had to keep going, keep moving, and never stop. If Daniel hadn't noticed the tracker wasn't working by now, he soon would.

Opening my eyes, I delved into my pocket and pulled out Frank's key. I dashed between the parked cars, clicking the button and looking for any flashing lights. Eventually, a Jeep Wrangler responded to my call.

I jogged towards it when a figure stepped out from behind a dark van four vehicles ahead, blocking my way to the car.

I didn't need to see a face to know it was Daniel.

My whole world came crashing in. I couldn't move... couldn't breathe. I'd made a stupid, stupid mistake.

"Hello, Thea. It's good to see you," he said as he walked toward me. "Though not quite the reunion I imagined." His lips tilted in a smile that made black spots swim in my vision.

He pulled something from his pocket that even in the poor light, I saw was a syringe.

Still, I couldn't move. My heart raced, and my breaths came so fast that I feared I'd hyperventilate and collapse before he reached me. Not that my fate would be better when he did.

"What, no greeting for your dear brother?" he asked.

"Hello, Daniel," I said, the words ringing hollow in ears overwhelmed by my own pulse.

He tilted his head to the side. "Is it not good to see me?"

"It's good to see you, Daniel. M-might I ask, what do you have in your hand?" I asked, although I knew the answer.

He stopped before me and lifted the syringe in front of my eyes. "This is ketamine. The same as last time. I am surprised you'd be so forgetful."

"Please, no. I don't want to. I'll come, but please?"

"Oh, dear, dear, Thea. If you didn't want to take the drug, you should never have left. Besides, it will make you happy. Don't you want to be happy?"

I shook my head, no, but Daniel reached out and grabbed my chin, digging his fingers in tight. "Don't worry," he said. "I can assure you any happiness will be short-lived." He grabbed my arm and pushed the sleeve of my T-shirt up onto my shoulder. "It's been fun playing this little game. Watching you sleep and run around in your own little world. But it's time we returned to the real world, don't you think?"

My mind was already too numb to wince when he pushed the needle into my bicep and pressed on the plunger.

"We should move while you still have full function of your limbs," he said as he pulled it out. "I don't think you'd like what would happen should I be forced to drag you."

My body buzzed like I had pins and needles all over, and nausea built in my stomach. Daniel gripped my hand, but it felt like his touch wasn't really there, like my hand had an outer layer five inches from the skin and it was that he grasped on to. I stepped forward, one foot after the other, but the floor moved, and I didn't know where my foot ended and it began.

"Thea," a voice sounded behind me as the word floated in bubbles around my head. "GET YOUR FUCKING HANDS OFF HER."

I giggled and tried to snatch the bubbles from the air before glancing at Daniel's face. It twisted and turned as his features distorted, but one thing was clear. For the first time in my life, I saw something other than anger, lust, and joy at my pain in his eyes. I saw fear.

I giggled some more and lifted my finger to point at his face. "You're in trouble," I said.

The words echoed back at me, louder and louder, filling my head. They floated in angry bubbles that tried to knock me off my feet.

"You're in trouble. You're in trouble." They no longer came to me in my own voice, but Daniel's. His face appeared angry and flushed in another bubble, then another and another. "You're in trouble," each head snarled.

I fell to my knees and tried to clasp my hands to my ears but couldn't reach them because of my outer layer. I sank into the ground as the pavement turned to spongy mush beneath me.

"You are not having a good day," my inner voice said in an

exasperated tone, and I broke into full-bellied laughter, unable to stop. Not even when I floated off the ground and drifted away in a bubble full of pins.

CHAPTER FIVE

Cane

"**G**ET YOUR FUCKING HANDS OFF HER." The words came out like a guttural roar.

Every muscle in my body corded, and I felt like I could run through a fucking wall to reach Thea.

The second I got off the phone with Rex, I'd charged upstairs to find her, only to discover her room empty, the door wide open. I should have checked it out before she went up. If anything happened to her...

Rex confirmed the battery still held power and, in all likelihood, had been charged within the last twelve hours. He estimated its maximum battery life at two to three days. That meant not only did the fucker know where she was, but he also had to have been in the same room as her on a regular basis.

I needed to get her the hell out of Midnight Anchor, now.

Leaving her room, I noted the window leading to the fire

escape open. As soon as I reached it, I saw some motherfucker stretch out and take her hand. I bellowed her name and practically jumped down the entire fire escape to reach her.

The slimy fucker had taken one look at me and legged it. I wanted to run after him and flay the skin from his fucking body before making him eat it, but Thea was behaving strangely. She was crying and laughing at the same time and snapping her hands in the air. She fell to the ground, clutching her ears, and I knew I could never leave her again. Three minutes away from her and I'd almost lost her.

I lifted her in my arms and carried her back to the bar.

She reached up and tickled my beard, still crying. She had a smile on her face, though the laughter subsided. "So soft and fluffy," she said, her words slurred. "Like Santa Claus. Are you going to give me a present?"

On the last word, her smile disappeared, and a look of horror came over her features. "No, please. I don't want a present. Don't give me a present." Her eyes darted from left to right as though she was seeing something only she could. "Don't give me a bad present," she echoed. "Promise me that you won't give me a bad present?"

I looked at her precious face and my heart melted. That fuck had messed with her big time and I was going to make him pay. "I promise," I said.

She rested her head on my chest and clamped her hand tight in my beard. "Thank you, Santa Cane," she murmured, before laughing again.

As soon as I kicked down the door to the bar, Cherrie spotted me and came running over. "What the hell's happened now?" she yelled above the music and voices. Bono and Lucky were there a hair's breadth later.

"Get everyone out," I said. "We're closed."

Lucky didn't hesitate. He went over to the jukebox, pulled the plug, and let out a loud whistle. While he threw everyone out, I ignored the screeching chairs, angry shouts, and bottles smashing — Lucky and Jameson could deal with that shit — and moved to the nearest couch with Cherrie and Bono hot on my heels.

"Don't leave me," Thea said as I laid her down.

"Sweetheart, I'm not going anywhere." I smiled and brushed the hair away from her face. I resisted the urge to brush away her tears, knowing they were never-ending. "Do you think you can let go of my beard?" I asked. "I think you might rip it from my face."

A pang of guilt hit me when her face flooded with panic. She frantically tried to withdraw her hand, but her fingers didn't seem to work the way they should. She was stuck fast, her grip like iron.

"Let me help," Cherrie said and knelt beside us, working each finger free.

"I'm sorry," Thea said. "I'm so sorry."

"Hey." I clasped her other hand. "You've got nothing to be sorry for, okay?" She looked so scared and lost, I wanted to bundle her in my arms and never let go. Instead, I turned to Bono. "You do anything about what that sick fuck gave her?"

Bono had been a medic in the Marines in his past life, something that came in handy far too often. Cherrie finished untangling her hand and stood to give him room. He checked Thea's pulse. "It's fast," he said. "Her breathing is too shallow. And from the way her eyes are darting about the place, I'd say she was hallucinating." He leaned in close and in his most calming voice asked, "Hey, sweetie. Can you tell me what you've taken?"

"No, don't make me. I don't want to do it." Thea clenched my hand tightly, and I tried to squeeze back in a reassuring manner.

Bono cursed and gave me a look that showed he was as pissed at this guy as I was. "No, sweetie," he said. "We'll never make you do it. We just need to know what it was so we can help you." Choosing his words with more care, he asked, "Can you tell me what you were given?"

She stared at him with a faraway look in her eyes. "You do not look like a veterinary surgeon," she said and laughed. "Do I look like a horse? Am I a horse?"

Her eyes darted around the bar, and her whole body went rigid. I tried to pull her hand to my chest to reassure her that everything would be okay. She just had to ride out the trip. But her arm was locked in place, and I worried if I pulled it too hard, it would snap.

Bono stood and paced behind me. "Fucking piece of shit," he said, his voice full of rage and concern that mirrored my own. "He's given her ketamine. From the way she's acting, I reckon it must have been a large, injected dose."

Thea let out a scream of anguish and then fell abruptly silent.

This wasn't the first time I'd seen someone on a bad trip. Hell, most of us had experienced one a time or two, but watching Thea's anguish and knowing there was not a goddamn thing I could do about it was making my blood boil. Even more so as I knew the fucker was still out there waiting to do worse. "How long before she comes down?" I asked.

"An hour. Maybe longer."

"Anything we can do?"

Bono shook his head. "Stay with her. Talk to her. Tell her where she is. Who she is." Easier said than done when we didn't have a clue. "She'll definitely experience hallucinations, panic, and confusion. The worse her state of mind going into the trip, the worse things will be, and I think it's safe to say she wasn't in a good fucking place."

No fucking kidding, Sherlock, I resisted saying and asked if there was anything else, instead.

"Dissociation. She may feel detached from her body and the things that are happening. This means that she won't feel pain, so we'll have to make sure she doesn't hurt herself."

"What kind of sick bastard does this to a person?" Cherrie asked.

I wished I had an answer. We weren't saints by any stretch of the imagination, but it would never cross our minds to put someone through this hell. My mind whirled. No wonder Thea was terrified of the fucker. If he'd done this to her without a moment's hesitation, what else was he capable of?

The next hour seemed to drag on longer than a full fucking day. Hell! From the range of emotions we all experienced along with Thea's anguished cries and bouts of frantic laughter, it might as well have been a fucking year.

Rex returned and started pacing.

"I think we should chuck the stupid bitch out on the street for her pimp to claim," Lucky said.

Growling, I clenched my spare fist.

Rex stopped in his tracks and took one look at me before turning to face Lucky. "And I think you should shut your stupid face before your luck runs out."

Lucky sucked in a breath. "Ah, shit. I didn't mean nothing by it. I just feel like I'm being tortured listening to this shit."

"Just watch your mouth," I said.

"We're all on edge." Rex started pacing again. "I need to be out of here, doing something. Ripping the fucker's limbs from his body."

Hell, I'd join him and hunt the fucker down, but my promise to Thea kept me firmly by her side.

After a few more minutes of pacing, Rex said he was going to check every bloody business within a one-mile radius to see if they had CCTV footage of the guy. I gave him a description and he left, along with Lucky who was more than eager to go with him.

"Rex," I shouted across the club before he left. "If you find the fucker, bring him back alive. You hear me?"

Rex nodded that he understood. I was gonna kill this goddamn piece of shit myself.

Thea never moved from the couch. For the last twenty minutes, she'd fallen silent, and in many ways that was worse than the laughing and crying. At least when she was doing those, we knew she was still alive. Only when she squeezed my hand did I let out a sigh of relief.

"My Santa Cane," she said and gave a short laugh, more

wistful than manic. She sobered quickly and reached out to touch my face. It was the first movement she'd made since going stiff. "You stayed," she said.

"I promised I would."

A sad smile slid into place. "I'm sorry."

"You never have to say those words to me again," I said. "You've got absolutely nothing to be sorry for."

"I should never have tried to run away from you. I just had to get away from the bar as fast as possible."

I tilted my head to the side. "Now that, you shouldn't have done, but I understand why you did. Just promise me you won't do it again."

"I promise," she said before wincing. "Everything hurts."

"Where?"

Her smile brightened and damn near lit up the whole fucking room. "Everywhere," she said, and I wondered what the hell she had to smile about, even through I couldn't help but smile in return.

CHAPTER SIX

Thea

I felt like I'd been dragged into hell, but always in the back of my mind, I knew that Cane was near me. I couldn't see his face, hear his voice, or feel his touch, but on some distant plane, he held my hand. Without that one thing to clutch on to, I don't think my mind would have ever made it back to my body.

Not that it felt great when it did. Spearing pain lanced through me as though my head had been pounded flat with a sledgehammer, and my body squished in a vice. I could almost wish to be free of it again, but that would mean losing sight of the man beside me. The one who'd never let go of my hand. I couldn't rationalize why I'd become so attached to a man I didn't know the first thing about. I just had.

An image of him dressed in nothing but a Santa hat and bottoms flashed in my mind, bringing a smile to my face. I couldn't remember much after running into Daniel, but I remembered Cane saving me and my calling him Santa Cane. He must think I'm an idiot. Which I was for believing I'd ever be free of Daniel.

One of Cane's brothers, the one with the close-cropped hair and a marine tattoo with the words '*Semper Fidelis*' tattooed on his forearm, introduce himself as Bono and gave me a couple of Advil to deal with my aches and pains. I drifted off to sleep as he and Cane discussed moving me away from the bar. Cherrie wasn't happy about me going anywhere without her, but conceded it would be best for me to stay with Cane, at least for a while.

"You got it bad for this girl?" Bono said to Cane, and I wondered what he meant. Though the idea Cane might like me filled my last thoughts with happiness and warmed my body before sleep claimed me.

~

When I awoke, I was in a pick-up truck with Cane driving.

He glanced my way as I shifted in the seat and gave me a warm smile. "How you feeling?" he asked.

"Better." Which was true. My body no longer felt as though it had been squished in a vice, but more achy like after a particularly tough yoga workout full of new poses.

The roar of engines drew my gaze out the rear window. Four bikes trailed behind us. The night was fast turning to day, and a wash of light from the east made me focus my attention on our surroundings. The new day sun reflected off the buildings, washing away the grayscale and flooding them with color. Soon, we moved away from the built-up area of the town and towards the mountains and surrounding forest.

"We're going to my place?" Cane gestured with his head to the bikes following. "They'll make sure nobody follows."

"Why?" We pulled off the main road into a tree-lined country lane. Two of the bikes gave us a honk of their horns and circled back on the road. Cane honked back. "I mean, why are you helping me? I've been nothing but a crazy mess since you met me."

He gave me a wry smile. "Maybe, that's why."

I looked to the floor and swallowed the lump forming in my throat. God, I must seem so weak and pathetic. All I wanted was to strip off his clothes, see how far those tattoos covered his body, and trace every line of them with my fingers. My tongue. He looked rough, ready, and dirty, and I wanted to do dirty things with him, but he only saw me as a charity case who needed saving, or worse, babying.

Involuntarily, my hand went to my throat to clutch the heart that until last night had always given me comfort. My chest tightened as a twang of disappointment at discovering it gone was quickly replaced by relief.

Who the hell was I kidding? I was pathetic and I did need saving.

I glanced back at the remaining two bikes.

"Rex and Jameson live in town," he explained noticing my look. "They'll be able to see if anyone was following on the trip back."

I nodded. Rex had been the one to identify the tracker, but I didn't have a clue which of the guys was Jameson.

"Lucky lives near the bar," Cane continued. "Says he misses the hustle and bustle out here in the sticks, but really he likes to stay with his Ma when he's in town, and make sure she's doing okay. He held back to watch the road out of town. Bono lives further on in the forest, not too far from me."

The lights from a cabin flashed by in the forest. I glanced back and noted the two bikes still following and counted the names off in my head. If Lucky had stayed behind, who was riding the fourth bike? Then it dawned on me. We were in Greg's pick-up, though the bike following wasn't the one I normally saw him ride.

"Is Greg on your bike?" I asked as Cane pulled up alongside a small cabin. One of the remaining bikes gave a toot and moved on, the other came to a stop behind us.

"He is." He turned off the engine and shifted to face me. "Can you walk?" he asked.

I nodded and moved to open the door, praying I was right. A

sigh of relief escaped my lips when I placed my first foot on the floor and found not only the ground solid but my leg able to take my weight.

The sun bathed the clearing in a warm glow as the fresh scent of pine needles enveloped my senses. The forest seemed alive with birds singing to welcome the new day. Dense foliage surrounded us, making me wonder how far I'd be able to see at night. The leaves rustled in a faint breeze and I tried not to shiver, uncertain about what or rather who might be watching in the dark depths.

Greg walked up and gave Cane a nod. "You doing alright, honey?" he asked, turning his attention to me.

"Thea," I said. "I'm sorry I lied."

Greg winked. "Hell, you did what you had to do. I just wish we'd known your problems sooner, so we could have helped you better."

"You've helped me far too much already."

"We ain't helped you enough." He nodded to Cane and patted him on the shoulder. "Though I reckon the brothers are gonna rectify that. Anyway," he handed Cane his bike keys and took his pick-up keys in return, "I'd better get back and help Cherrie clean up and get some rest before the bar opens tonight. You need the slightest thing, you just call and ask, you hear?"

"Yes, sir, and thank you."

He winked again and jumped in the truck before pulling away, leaving me standing in the clearing with Cane.

"Are they all your brothers?" I asked just to say something when a fluttery feeling settled in my stomach.

"They are."

I cleared my throat. "They don't look much like you. Are they brothers by birth or by marriage?"

Cane bellowed a hearty laugh and flashed me a smile that somehow softened his whole gruff exterior. "Neither, they're brothers in heart and soul," he said. "We're all members of the Forever Midnight Motorcycle Club, but the club is more than just that. We love each other, support each other. Hell, every one of the brothers would lay down their lives for each other. We're true family."

My heart sank to my stomach at his words. My family had never been about love, compassion or support. Not since Dad had died. Although, Mom was right in one aspect. I was only eight when that happened. Maybe I viewed my time with him through rose-tinted spectacles. More so after the family that came next.

Sensing my discomfort, Cane glanced from me to the cabin and suggested we go in. "I'm fucking starving," he said. "I ain't got much in. We've been on the road the past two months, and the place could probably use airing. But there'll be a can of soup or some shit to eat in one of the cupboards."

I smiled and bit my lip. Only Mom ever swore around me, and that was infrequent. Tony hated a potty mouth. But every other word that came out of Cane's mouth, was f-ing this or f-ing that. It seemed crass yet adorable at the same time. Every time he said *fuck,* I wanted to do just that.

My face felt flushed when I stepped up onto the decking and he opened the door, ushering me inside. I glanced around. Two chairs sat either side of a fireplace. There was a table and chairs next to an open plan kitchen, and a spiral staircase leading up to a mezzanine, where I could just see the makings of a bed.

"The bathroom's through that door to the back," he said, pointing past the kitchen and to the far wall. "There's only the one bed. I'll get some bedding for you and—"

"What about you?" I asked. "Where will you sleep?" He gestured to the chairs by the fireplace.

I huffed out a breath, shocked at the disappointment that washed over me. From habit, I took off my boots and socks — I wasn't allowed to wear them at home — left them by the door and moved to the kitchen area afraid to say out loud the thought that popped into my head. He joined me and opened a cupboard, pulling out a couple of cans.

"Looks like there's beans, corn, and tuna," he said. "Beans okay?"

"What? No shit?" I asked and raised an eyebrow.

He quirked his lips and sized me up and down making me feel warm and tingly. "Don't be judging the quality of the beans or my cooking skills too soon," he said.

I laughed. "I'm not sure heating beans counts as cooking."

He crossed his arms, gave me a stern look, and pressed his lips together. I could imagine how intimidating it would be if he'd turned the same look on someone else, but it just made me laugh even harder. "I have to open the can and heat the contents," he said in earnest.

"Oh, that's right. I stand corrected. Just be careful not to burn them. I'm starving and could eat a horse."

He stiffened and placed the cans too carefully on the countertop. The muscles in his neck corded the way they had the night before. When he looked as though he might punch the cupboard door the way I'd seen some men on the TV do, I wondered if I'd overstepped my mark and said the wrong thing. But something told me his anger wasn't directed my way. After a moment, he got control of whatever emotions warred inside him and opened a drawer before pulling out a can opener.

"There's some bowls over there," he said, motioning to another cupboard.

I sighed, sorry that my careless words had changed the atmosphere between us, grabbed the bowls, and placed them next to the stove, while Cane emptied the beans into a pan and heated them.

"I'm sorry. I didn't mean to sound ungrateful. Beans are perfect and more than enough."

He took in a deep breath before huffing it out. "It's not the beans. Last night, you wondered if Bono was a veterinary surgeon and you were a horse."

Oh, and I'd just said I could eat a horse.

I racked my brain trying to remember what else I'd done or said last night, but nothing came. Only the image of Daniel standing before me, and I never wanted to think about that again. I pushed his face aside and focused on Cane's. "I'm sorr—"

"You really fucking have to stop apologizing."

I bit my tongue to stop myself from apologizing for apologizing and asked where the spoons were instead. Cane pointed to a drawer and then poured the heated beans into the two bowls before taking them over to the table.

We ate in silence. Although I tried not to stare, I couldn't keep my eyes off of Cane. Everything about him seemed intense. His beard, and tattoos. His broad shoulders and chest. Not to mention his arms as big as tree trunks. I pictured myself running at him full force and falling flat on my back without causing him to huff out a breath. He was enormous, and easily the sexiest guy alive. One glance and I could tell he knew exactly how to use his powerful body and had the stamina to go all night. The thought of my bare skin touching his made my heart skip a beat. My every sense tingled with a mixture of anticipation and fear. But I wasn't afraid. Not of him.

After he finished eating, he placed his spoon in his bowl and sat back in the chair, crossing his arms in front of his chest again. From the look he gave me, I knew I wouldn't like what was coming next. "At some point, we're gonna need to talk about what happened," he said. "About who that fucker was."

"I know." Although I'd been starving and still had some beans in my bowl, my appetite fled, and I placed my spoon down too. "The man who… who—"

"The one from last night. He your pimp or something?"

I gave him a wry smile. "The one from last night. His name is Daniel. Daniel King. He's my stepbrother."

It felt fine to talk about him at that moment; I was still slightly detached from reality; the one benefit of the ketamine he'd given me. The only thing that seemed real and made me feel alive was the way Cane looked at me.

He tensed his fists until his knuckles whitened, and the muscles in his arms twitched. "He give you the tracker?" he asked.

Despite my numbness, I held back the tears that threatened to flow and shook my head. "That was a present from my Mom.

The last gift she ever gave me." I stood and took my bowl to the kitchen area.

Cane appeared beside me. My hand flew to my mouth, and I released a sob. I was so stupid, so pathetic. Nothing could stop the tears as they fell now, and without thinking, I leaned into Cane, wanting more than anything for him to wrap his arms around me and make everything okay. He did, and we stayed like that for countless minutes, neither of us moving or saying a word. Only when I felt the stirring of his cock did my tears subside. I lifted my head and looked into his deep brown eyes, willing him to make a move.

"You must be tired," he said, drawing back. "We should get some rest."

CHAPTER SEVEN

Cane

Fuck!

I needed a cold shower or something. Thea was distraught, and all I could think about was how perfect she felt in my arms. How tight she'd feel around my cock.

When I felt my thick cock getting hard, I pulled away and suggested we get some rest, but fuck if I didn't picture throwing her down on the bed and burying my head in her delightful pussy.

In any other situation, I'd do just that.

When she looked up at me, her eyes were dripping with desire. She stepped back, bit her lip, and removed her jeans before kicking them across the floor.

My gaze focused on her demure mouth. I sure as hell knew where I wanted it to go.

Oh, fuck me, woman. What the hell are you doing to me?

I growled, wanting to explore every inch of her, and from the way she acted, I knew for certain my touch wasn't unwanted. Still, I'd promised Cherrie, *'Not an unwanted finger'*. The thought made me want to plunge my fingers deep inside her, but still, I had to be sure.

"What do you want?" I asked.

She backed against the wall and pulled me towards her. In nothing but that stupid oversized T-shirt, she looked every inch the most fuckable thing on the planet.

She moved her head close and brushed her lips against mine. "I want you."

Fuck me!

All trace of innocence disappeared, and a fuck-goddess replaced it.

CHAPTER EIGHT

Thea

When Cane had suggested we get some rest, the only thing I wanted to do was have him in that bed with me. Although, I didn't think I could wait to get him upstairs. I'd felt the bulge in his pants. The size of his erection as it skimmed my belly. I needed to know what it felt like.

I kicked my jeans across the floor as he stood staring at my mouth. God, I needed to know what he tasted like.

When he growled, a predatory smile played on his lips, and a thrill rushed through my body, making me want to scream and demand that he do whatever he wanted to me.

"What do you want?" he asked as though it wasn't obvious.

The brush of my lips against his somehow made my core tingle. "I want you," I answered.

It seemed an eternity before he gently ran his fingers along my chin and brushed my lips. Heat pulsed between my legs.

I opened my mouth, wanting him to push them inside, but instead, he filled it with his tongue. I lost myself in his sweet taste of honey and beans. His earthy scent made me think his wild home reflected his wild nature.

I shuddered, and Cane pushed against me, tight, pinning me to the wall. I felt the beat of his heart through the contact. The silky softness of his lips and the tickle of his beard stood in sharp contrast to the feel of his chiseled chest beneath my hands. I wanted to feel the touch of his bare flesh.

I tried to speak, but lost all ability when he pushed his knee between my legs.

His tongue probed my mouth. The muscles in my core clenched in need. I wasn't pure. My virginity was the one thing I made sure Daniel could never take from me. But that one time was terrifying. I'd been a shy, nervous wreck. Now, my body ached intensely for Cane's touch. I wanted him too bad to feel nervous about what I was doing.

He grasped my hair and pulled it back, before dipping to my neck and breathing me in. Fire flooded through my veins, and blood roared through my ears. "You're mine," he said as though claiming me.

Yes, I am!

His lips trailed down my neck, and my temperature spiked. I'd been hot before, but now I felt like a volcano about to erupt.

I sensed his power as a low growl built in his chest and the need between my legs grew heavier.

Firm hands gripped my arms and pinned them above my head. Cane kissed my mouth, my neck; he nipped at my earlobe. His warm breath caressed my skin as his beard tickled it. He pushed the hardness of his cock against me.

I ached to release it from the burden of his leather pants, but with my hands above my head all I could do was let out a low frustrated growl of my own. His one hand enveloped both of mine, keeping them in place. The other reached under my T-shirt and beneath my bra.

"You are so fucking perfect," he said, making me blush.

Trembling, I bit my lip to keep from crying out, while Cane brushed his thumb in a slow circle over my nipple. Both tightened in anticipation.

I imagined him sucking them into his mouth while his cock slid between my folds. My core clenched, wishing there was something to clench against. His cock, his fingers, anything. I couldn't take it anymore; I needed to feel him inside me, not more teasing. I tried to pull away from the wall and reach towards him, but he pushed me back, brought his mouth to my ear and whispered, "Don't move."

With that, he pulled back, panting, and I realized his need was as great as mine. His long dark eyelashes fluttered against his cheeks, fanning my desire as his eyes devoured my lips. My body trembled with a need so great I thought my legs would buckle beneath me. I resisted the urge to lower my arms or close my eyes, afraid that the slightest movement would make Cane disappear, and I'd discover his presence was nothing but a dream.

Inch by agonizing inch, he pulled my T-shirt and bra over my head, wrapped them around my wrists, binding my arms before, once again, pinning them above my head. I closed my eyes as his other hand moved to the band of my panties.

I moaned, urging him to go lower. "I've wanted to do this since you first fucking walked into the room at the bar," he said, before touching me where I needed him to most. He circled my clit, making me twitch and squirm with need. "All I want to do is put my hard fucking wood in your pussy and pound until you scream in release."

A wave of nervous energy flushed through me, and I trembled at his words. He pulled his hand away, leaving me bereft, and pushed my panties to the floor. I stood pinned against the wall, naked before him, while he stood fully dressed before me. Hardly fair, in the circumstance. Not when I wanted to look at his perfect form.

I felt exposed in a way I never had before. Goosebumps rose on my skin and my nipples tightened. Noticing, he teased the taught buds with his tongue, moving from one breast to the other. I arched into him.

"I need you," I said.

He looked up at me for a second before taking my nipple into his mouth and sucking hard, causing a tsunami of sensation to explode inside me.

"Oh, God." I groaned and tried to catch my breath. Cane responded by nipping and sucking on my bud until I couldn't stand it any longer and said as much between panted breaths.

His lips twitched in a smile as he looked at me and slid his hand over my mound. He teased my clit. My pulse beat between my legs like a war drum. I wanted to reach out, and grab onto his hard body, but didn't move my hands as he teased at my entrance.

"You're so fucking wet for me," he said with no hint of surprise in his voice. I gasped as he pushed two fingers inside me.

My core clenched around his fingers as they slid deep within me, moving faster and faster, building the friction I needed to find release.

"Tell me what you want?" he asked as he pumped my sopping core and circled my clit with his thumb. Pleasure built. I arched into his fingers. "Tell me what you want?" he said again, almost growling the words.

I could never have imagined a man could give without taking. I'd not laid a hand on Cane. He'd spent all this time playing with me, and now he asked what I wanted. He couldn't be real.

"More," I groaned.

Cane stopped, withdrew his fingers, and kissed my mouth deeply. "What do you want?" he asked again.

"I want you." My eyes rested on the giant bulge in his leather pants. "Please."

Cane unfastened his pants, and his cock sprang free, sending an extra ripple of pleasure flooding to my core.

"Fuck Me," I said and hissed in a breath at the size of him. "That is never going to fit." His cock was at least ten inches, as hard as steel, and to my eyes at that moment seemed as thick as his arms. I couldn't take my eyes off it.

Cane smiled. "That's the plan, and yes, it is. You're mine, remember? Which means you're fucking made for me and me for you." He lined himself up and teased his bulbous head against my entrance.

My core twitched. He lifted me slightly. Trembling, I shifted my hips closer to his, pleading for him to spear me. My heart felt as though it knocked against my ribcage, but still, he teased, moving forward little by little with agonizing slowness, before withdrawing.

I wanted to howl in frustration, but "I need... I need..." was all that came out.

With each movement, he stretched me to fit him. Again and again, he pushed inside. Until, at last, a surge of pleasure blasted through me when he impaled me with one complete thrust.

"Oh God," I moaned as my core finally clenched around his full hardness. Cane lifted one of my legs and then the other, wrapping them around his waist. He slipped his hands around my bottom.

He traced fiery kisses down my neck as he pummeled into me hard and fast, driving my backside against the wall. My breath caught and my heart beat so fast, I thought it might jump right out of my body. Still, he pumped into me, pinning me against the wall.

"Fuck, woman! You're the most perfect woman I've ever laid my eyes on," he said. "I want to fuck you all day and all night long."

"What's stopping you?" I never wanted this to end.

He growled, and although I didn't think it was possible, plunged deeper. I cried out and dropped my bound hands over his head. I was coming apart and nothing could stop me. I lifted my hips asking for more, and he gave it.

I quivered. My eyes rolled to the back of my head and my muscles clamped around his cock. I convulsed with pleasure.

"Oh, fuck," I gasped.

"I love it when you fucking cuss," he said and claimed my lips, hard and fast, the way his cock claimed my core.

He buried himself deep inside, and my senses went into overdrive, igniting my whole body with fiery delight. The sparks of pleasure building within my core exploded, and black dots danced in front of my eyes, but Cane didn't stop. Holding me in place, he pounded into me. I clung to his head, pulling it to my breast and shuddered out my pleasure. My core spasmed and pulsed, milking his cock until animalistic moans escaped his lips.

He pulled out, spilling his seed on my stomach, then rested his head on my bosom and panted. After a moment, he lifted it and looked at me. "You are fucking unbelievable," he said and kissed me again. "Fuck am I ever letting you go."

CHAPTER NINE

Cane

This woman was everything. Her warm pussy welcomed my cock and hugged it nice and tight. I gave it to her good and hard, but even after I bathed her in my seed, I needed more. I needed to taste her.

With her hands still bound behind my head, I grabbed onto her ass to keep her legs wrapped around my waist and spun her around.

She squealed, and a look of delight flushed her face. Her perfect round tits pushed against my chest, and I wished for all the world, I'd taken my clothes off so I could feel them against my bare skin. But I'd been too needy to wait.

I took her over to the rug by the fire, laid her down, and unbound her hands after unhooking them from my head. I wanted her fingers to trace every part of my body. Standing, I took off my jacket and T-shirt before using the T-shirt to mop up the remainder of my cum from her stomach. Her eyes kept drifting to my cock, and the thought of me plunging it into her again made me instantly hard.

Leaving her lying on the floor, I stood over her and removed the rest of my clothing, kicking off my boots and pants. She bit her bottom lip in the most adorable fucking way as she watched me wide-eyed.

A growl escaped my lips. "I'm gonna make you come so fucking much, you're gonna beg me to stop."

"Promises. Promises," she said as though challenging me.

A huge motherfucking grin split my face. I was more than up to the challenge.

She moaned as I pushed her legs open and revealed her pussy in all its perfect glory. "Fuck. I bet you taste as good as you look," I said and kneeled between her legs.

She raised an eyebrow and reached for my thick cock. "I've been thinking the same thing about you."

My cock twitched just thinking about having those pouty lips wrapped around it, but I pushed her hand away. "Me first."

She laughed and it seemed as though my dingy cabin filled with light. I spread her legs further apart and lowered my head. Her breath hitched, making me smile again, and goosebumps rose on her flesh where my beard touched. I couldn't wait to see how her body reacted to my tongue.

"I'm gonna eat you out until you squirt."

"More promises," she said, feigning boredom.

I nipped at the inside of her thigh, and she yelped, but her legs moved further apart. "You like that," I said and nipped her again before pulling apart her folds and running my tongue up and down her slit.

She was so wet and ready for me again. But the taste... Fuck. She tasted so good. Like sweet apple pie and cream. I flicked my tongue over her clit and sucked it in. Her fingers threaded through my hair, making me glad I hadn't cut it short.

I sucked slowly at first. Her clit pulsed and twitched in my mouth. She moaned. I growled. Every part of me wanted to be inside her again, to feel her pulse around my cock, but I resisted, kept my touch light, and circled her clit slowly with my tongue until she writhed beneath me.

Her grip on my hair tightened, and she tried to pull my head up. "I can't... I can't..." she said, breathless.

I licked harder and probed her pussy with the tip of my tongue. She arched her back lifting her bottom from the ground, begging me for more friction. I pushed down on her stomach to hold her in place. I said I'd make her squirt, and she was gonna.

I slid my hand between her legs and pulled her clit into my mouth while plunging my fingers into her pussy. Two, three.

"Oh God," she gasped while I relentlessly finger-fucked her.

I released her clit from my mouth, rubbed it with the pad of my thumb, and lifted my head to look at her. Her head arched back, but her eyes never left mine. I smiled and shifted my fingers to hold her like a six-pack.

Her mouth opened in a delicious fucking 'O' as my middle finger delved into her butt hole. My index finger worked her pussy and my thumb rubbed against her clit. Her eyes rolled into the back of her head, and she writhed her hips to meet my fingers.

"Cane," she screamed. "It's too much, too much." Sweat soaked her skin.

"It's not fucking enough." I dipped my head and pulled her tight nipple into my mouth, and sucked, while my fingers covered all the bases.

A spasm racked her body, and her pussy pulsed against my finger, but I wasn't through with her yet. I withdrew my fingers and speared her with my cock, riding out her orgasm with her.

I spent the rest of the day taking her any and every way I could. In every part of my small cabin. Claiming her as mine. I didn't know what the hell it was about this woman, but I wanted her to compare every other guy she'd fuck in her life with me and find them wanting. I wanted to fuck her so much that she'd never get my stench off. She couldn't walk straight by the time I'd finished with her.

It was late afternoon when shut-eye claimed her. Her eyes drifted closed, and no matter how hard she tried, she couldn't open them again.

I smoothed a trail down her back as she lay naked on my bed. She murmured softly, and I pulled her into me, letting her feel my hardness against her ass. Her legs entangled in my own, and she moaned.

I brushed her hair from her neck and nuzzled it with kisses. "I'm gonna fuck you again when you wake up," I said.

She giggled. "Promises. Promises."

CHAPTER TEN

Cane

I woke at around ten that night, dying for a drink. Leaving Thea in bed, I edged down the stairs, smiling when I saw everywhere I'd taken her. It felt so fucking good being inside her, and I wanted to do it again and again. After using the bathroom and getting cleaned up, I resisted the urge to run upstairs for another round, and rooted around in my cupboards, found some coffee, and turned the coffee machine on.

Besides the fact that Midnight Anchor had opened three hours ago, and I'd likely be getting calls asking for a fucking update, the woman had a truck load of issues, and I wasn't sure I wanted her getting too attached. I wasn't looking to settle down and get me an old lady. Even if a part of me never wanted to let her go.

Plus, I'd promised her a fuck when she woke up and I wasn't about to renege on that promise.

As I waited for the coffee machine to percolate, my thoughts drifted to the fucker who'd hurt her. Not a mark scarred her perfect body, so he'd never beaten her too badly. But he'd done a fucking number on her mental state.

If anything, when she'd said he was her stepbrother, I wanted the fucker to pay for what he'd done even more. When I caught him, and I would catch him, I was gonna make him wish he'd never been born. Everything I did was for my brothers, my family. Even as a stepbrother, he was supposed to look out for Thea, not fuck her up.

My neck muscles twitched, the way they did when I got real fucking angry. Without thinking, I pulled two mugs from the cupboard and slammed them on the counter before pouring Thea a cup along with my own.

What the fuck had this woman done to me? She had me waiting on her hand and foot. Next time, she could make the coffee.

I picked up the first mug and felt a presence behind me. A rush of adrenaline flooded my body. I dropped the mug, and raised my fist, turning to pummel whoever the fuck was there.

My fist froze in mid-air. Thea looked at me wide-eyed and cleared her throat. "Sorry," she said. "I um—"

"Fuck, woman. I could have killed you." I huffed and clenched my fists trying to get my surge of testosterone under control.

A sad smile played on her lips, and she took a step back. Damn, she looked so fucking vulnerable with nothing but a bed sheet wrapped around her. I'll be damned if a wave of guilt didn't hit me like a ton of bricks.

I wanted nothing more than to pull her into my arms, or better yet rip the damn sheet right off and eat her out again. She'd soon forget her troubles.

She must have seen the tension leave my body and the need to fuck her rise, as her gaze flicked down to my cock now standing to attention before shifting to the dropped mug and the spilled coffee, and then back again.

"I made you some coffee," I said, although it had to be the worst fucking apology in history.

"Thanks." A shy smile played at the edge of her lips and she moved a step closer. "I take mine in a cup."

I ran my hand over my head and tried to think of a comeback, but with my mind focused on all the dirty things we'd done together and all the possibilities we still had to explore, words failed me. In the end, the best I could muster was, "In that case, I got you covered." I lifted the second mug and handed it to her.

Thea laughed. A full, chiming giggle that was both unexpected and surprisingly musical. It brought a smile to my face.

I brushed her long hair over her shoulder, took the mug from her hand before laying it back on the counter, and pulled her close. I took my time with the kiss that followed, savoring her flavor and the way she felt in my arms.

After a moment, she pulled her head away and looked up into my face. "I need to wash up," she said. "I must stink."

"You smell fucking gorgeous." She did. Like sex and heat.

She raised an eyebrow and smiled. "I smell like I need a shower." My cell buzzed and vibrated on the kitchen counter. Thea's face dropped, and she pulled back. "I'll go take a shower."

I patted her ass as she walked away. "I'll join you in a minute. I'm pretty sure I promised you something when you woke up."

Thea blushed and looked at her feet as though she was shy and not the same fucking woman who rode my cock half the day.

"This better be good," I said into the phone as soon as she closed the bathroom door.

"My thoughts exactly," Caleb answered. "I was about to send Bono to break down your fucking door. I've been calling for hours."

I leaned against the kitchen counter, ran my hand over my head, and closed my eyes. "It's been a long day and my phone was on vibrate."

"And what's your excuse for taking Cherrie's pet project back to your place? She got some nice fucking tits or something?" A low growl built in my chest and my body tensed. "You were meant to talk some sense into Cherrie, and have the girl turfed out on the street, but instead I hear you rescued the stupid drugged-up whore from her pimp. Hell, I'll bet—"

"You wanna come say that to my FUCKING FACE?" I held my phone so tight the screen crackled as though fit to burst.

"Who the *hell* do you think you're talking to? I'LL TATTOO IT ON YOUR FUCKING ASS!"

Neither of us said anything and the silence that stretched along the line could cut stone. Eventually, I huffed out a breath and Caleb did the same.

"Bro," Caleb said after a moment. "Bono told me you liked her. He didn't tell me you had it this bad."

"I ain't got shit bad." Even as the words left my mouth, I wondered how true they were.

"Good. Then use her like a dolly girl," he said, using the name we called the women we fucked as though they were blow-up dolls. "Fuck her senseless and get her out of your Goddamn system. Shits about to get real interesting with the Feral Sons, and I need you focused with your head in the game. As soon as you're done, you can buy her a one-way ticket away from her pimp as payment."

I clenched my jaw along with my fists. "She's not a whore.

You call her a Goddamn whore one more time—"

"Then who was the guy last night and why the hell should I care if she's a whore or not? For that matter, why the hell do you care?"

Goddamnit! Why the hell did I care? Just hearing him talk about Thea like that made my blood boil, and there was no way in hell, I could let it slide.

"That sick fucker last night was her stepbrother. Daniel King, I think she said his name was." Caleb fell silent, but I could feel his tension emanating along the line. "You've heard that name before," I said more as a statement than a question.

"I think I might have. If it's the guy I'm thinking of, sick fuck would be an understatement."

"You got an address on this fucker?"

"Just… just leave it with me for now. I'll check in with you tomorrow morning. Until then, do as I said. Use her like a dolly girl and get her out of your goddamn system."

Caleb ended the call without saying anything else. I held my cell to my forehead for a moment. What the hell was this woman doing to me? I wasn't after no old lady.

I slammed my phone on the counter and moved to the bathroom door. The sound of the shower greeted me when I edged it open. Thea didn't notice me at first. I watched through the steamy air as she bathed in the cascading water. Long, brown hair clung to her body all the way down to an ass, so delicious and round, I couldn't stop staring at it. She turned slightly. Droplets sluiced from her pert nipples, down her belly, and towards her mound.

I growled. Caleb was right, I needed to fuck her until I was tired of looking at that perfect pussy. Though, I couldn't imagine such a time would ever come.

CHAPTER ELEVEN

Thea

My day with Cane had been crazy. I'd acted like a woman possessed and could barely imagine myself ever doing the things I'd done. If it wasn't for the ache between my thighs, I'd shrug it off as a drug-fueled dream. Though I had no doubt the drugs within my system played a part in how I'd acted.

The hot stream of water cleansed my body, but it did little to cleanse the thoughts from my mind as I imagined tracing my hands along the tattoos that covered Cane's upper body before kneeling and sucking on his cock. Just the word cock sounded out of place in my thoughts. What the hell was wrong with me?

A guttural growl drew my attention to the door, and my breath hitched. Cane stood watching me, still naked, and with a feral look in his eyes.

He charged forward, stopping a foot away from me. A splatter of water from the shower hit his face and streamed from his eyelashes, but he didn't blink. He just looked at me as though I was a piece of meat to devour.

"Do you want me?" he asked and trailed the back of his thumb across my lip.

God help me, I did. "Yes."

Without another word, he pinned me to the wall and lifted my legs. An explosion of need shot to my core. He tangled his fingers in my hair and yanked my head back so that it faced the ceiling. Water blasted my face, and I had to close my eyes.

The next thing I knew, he thrust some fingers on his other hand inside me. "Always fucking ready," he murmured into my ear as his beard tickled my shoulder.

He removed his fingers and lifted me from the ground. I wound my legs around him. There was no teasing this time, no gentle stretching. His cock found my entrance and thrust to the hilt inside. I cried out in a mixture of pain and pleasure. He continued pulling on my hair, keeping my head back as he thrust in and out, rougher than he ever had before. His mouth found the crook of my neck and licked up to my ear.

"Do you want me?" he asked again.

"Y-yes. Please," I said.

My body became undone at his touch. Needing, begging for everything he gave me, even though in the back of my mind, I questioned if we should stop.

Something was different. Something in Cane had changed, and I wondered what had happened on the phone call.

My arms gripped his shoulders as tightly as my legs clamped around him. My whole body trembled. He grunted and continued his relentless thrusts, hard, fast and so deep, I feared his cock would pierce me from the inside through my navel.

I wanted to look at him and see the thoughts playing on his face, but he fought against me and tightened his grip on my hair.

Still, his cock filled me, building the friction I needed to climax. Fire gathered, and his cock sent shuddering waves of pleasure rippling through my core. All the air ripped from my lungs and my blood pounded in my ears. I screamed as my body took me over the edge and wave after wave of pleasure imploded within me. Still, Cane didn't stop. He drove into me, over and over.

After a moment, he stilled. A shudder racked his body, but his cock still resided rock-hard inside me.

He released my hair, pulled my head down, and rested his forehead against mine. Water gushed around our faces and steam filled the small bathroom.

"God, why are you so fucking perfect," he said.

"I could ask you the same thing?" Trying to lighten his mood, I clenched my core around his cock and raised an eyebrow. A smile played on his lips. "You like that, do you?" I asked and did it again.

He laughed. "How the hell did I ever survive without you?" he asked, before pulling his cock back and teasing the head at my entrance, getting me ready to go again.

~

Cane made another cup of coffee and ordered a pizza. He sat down in one of the chairs by the fireplace and pulled me into his lap. I wore nothing but one of his T-shirts. His top was bare, so I studied the tattoos covering his chest, paying particular attention to the one over his heart. It depicted a skull with wings coming out of it and a full moon in the background.

"Forever Midnight." I traced the letters of the words accompanying the design with my fingers. "You said that was the name of your motorcycle club."

"I did."

When he didn't elaborate, I smiled. "Aren't they all supposed to be called Sons of Death, Demons of the Dark, or… I don't know, Blades of Glory or something?"

He twitched his lips and let out a grunt. "Blades of Glory is a movie." He pulled me in closer and kissed me on the lips, deep and hard, probing my mouth with his tongue. "Although now I think about it, I also heard it was a sex act," he said when he pulled away.

"It is not." I nudged him in the ribs with my elbow and

rolled my eyes. "But seriously, why Forever Midnight and not something badass like Midnight Fury or something?"

"Like Midnight Fury sounds fucking badass..." His words trailed off and he stared out the window, his gaze going distant.

What little I could see of the night sky showed the moon hanging bright and flooding out the possibility of stars. A gentle wind shook the branches of the surrounding trees, rustling their leaves. I resisted a shudder. It wasn't the unknown in the forest that should frighten me. There were plenty of real things to fear.

I pushed away the dark thoughts that threatened to surface, and stroked my hand down his chest, over the six-pack beneath. Scars lined his body. One just below his waist was dark and dipped in. Given its shape, I wondered if it could be a bullet wound. I ran the tips of my fingure over it and Cane turned his head to look at me. The lines on his face were serious.

"I'm not a good man," he said. "I know you think I am, but I'm not."

I sighed. The truth was, neither of us knew the first thing about each other, and this brief chat was the longest conversation we'd had since meeting. Not that we'd had much chance to talk.

Sexually, I couldn't think of something I hadn't done with Cane, well... besides tasting his cock, although he assured me otherwise.

I frowned, wondered if Blades of Glory really was a sex act, and if so what it would entail. I then had to stifle a laugh when all I pictured was a lot of arms and legs wearing roller blades slipping all over the place and going every which way.

There was no doubt, I'd reacted to his physical presence and the depth of emotions I saw in Cane's eyes even before he rescued me from Daniel. From the moment I walked into the back room to take his order, my body had needed him. There was an undeniable chemistry between us, like some raw animal need, but was there anything other than sex? I'd be damned if I knew. Besides, what was I expecting? To stay locked up in his cabin forever, having sex and pretending that the outside world didn't exist? Sure, it would be fun for a day or two, or even three, but eventually, reality would kick in. As it was, I only had the clothes I'd arrived in, which were now washed and drying outside, very little money, and there was no food in the house.

"My dad started the club and named it Forever Midnight," Cane said, breaking his silence. His gaze once again stared out the darkened window and into the shadows beyond. "He used to say there was no better time of day. When the stars were over head or the moon was full, whichever. He said that a sense of peace comes over the world, and just for a second, he liked to get off his bike, look at the open road surrounding him and look to the sky. At that moment, no matter what other crap was going on, everything was okay, because it all meant shit anyway." His eyes met mine and he huffed out a breath. "He named the club Forever Midnight because he wished he could stay in that moment forever."

It was hard to respond to that. I didn't know if it was beautiful or tragic. Though, I feared it was the latter. "He used to?"

"He died a little over three years back. Got knifed in a bar fight. Stupid fucked up way to go and he should have known better."

"Did they catch whoever did it?"

Cane nodded. "We did. My blood-brother Caleb and me." From the way he said the words, I had little trouble imagining what he and his brother did to the person responsible.

"My dad died, too. When I was eight. He had cancer. It was just Mom and me for a while after that. Things weren't great, but she remarried when I was twelve and they got even worse."

"How worse?"

"I first ran away when I was sixteen. I didn't make it very far." I scoffed and shook my head. "Mom knew I needed to escape and get away, that's when she gave me the tracker. I'd been so stupid to trust her. All this time… I tried five more times after that. I was even stupid enough to try and run away to college. I mean, who does that?"

My voice stilled and my body tensed as though a great weight rested on my chest. Mom had been so different when Dad was alive. She never drank or took drugs. She always had a smile, even on a bad day.

Cane squeezed my hand. "My Mom was a bitch too. Ran out on us a year or so after I was born."

"I'm sorry."

"Don't be. She was a fucking waste of space. We were well rid of her. Dad and Caleb raised me, along with my brothers in the club."

A car engine sounded in the distance and gravel crunched beneath its tires. Cane rose and stood me on my feet before pushing me behind him. Holding my hand, he edged to the window being sure to stay out of view. My heart raced, and I worried Daniel had found us.

"Pizza's here," Cane said and smiled before moving to the kitchen to fetch his money.

I sat perched on the edge of the chair, unsure what to do with myself while he answered the door.

"That smells so good," I said as I breathed in the delicious scent of cheese and tomato.

Cane tossed the box on the table, along with a bottle of cola he'd ordered with the pizza, and opened it up. He took a deep breath in through his nose and smiled. "It sure does." He lifted a piece and took a bite. "I feel like I haven't eaten for a week," he said between mouthfuls.

I joined him and grabbed a piece of my own. To say the first bite was heavenly would be an understatement.

The next few minutes were consumed with silence. The only sounds were appreciative grunts at the much-needed food that warmed our bellies. I was done after three slices, but Cane went on to finish the entire extra-large 16" pizza, complete with mushrooms and pepperoni.

When he'd finished, he sat back in his chair and stretched his arms above his head before rubbing his tummy.

"I should have ordered two," he said. "We might have had some leftovers for breakfast then."

I glanced around the room looking for a clock. "When is breakfast? Other than to say it's night, I have no idea what time it actually is."

Cane moved to the kitchen and looked at his phone. "A little after two. Midnight Anchor will be kicking out now."

I nodded and wondered at the relationship Cane had with Cherrie and Greg at the bar. Though it was clear now that Greg was a member of their motorcycle club. I closed the pizza box, carried the rubbish to the kitchen, and glanced around the simple cabin. The furniture was sparse, there was no TV, and while everything was in good working order, it wasn't exactly high-end. I liked it. Nice and simple without ostentation. "Cherrie called you the owners of Midnight Anchor," I said. "Is that what you do for a living?"

I worried that Cane would become annoyed at my constant questions, but what else was there to do? We'd had our fill of both food and sex, well... at least it seemed as though we'd reached a natural lull in the latter, for now, and with no other source of entertainment, conversation was our best bet.

It seemed silly to think of me as the conversation starter when I'd tried to be as quiet as possible and not attract any attention to myself for years. It seemed even more silly that I wasn't afraid of Cane. Even after he said he wasn't a good man, a small voice inside my head told me he was better than he realized. Although maybe I'd seen the worst of people in Daniel and anyone, by comparison, would seem like a saint.

"Forever Midnight owns the bar," Cane said and leaned against the counter taking a swig of cola from the bottle before offering it to me. "That includes Greg and all the other brothers."

The bar was busy, but I couldn't imagine it providing enough income for the few brothers I'd seen. "Is that all you do?" I asked, wanting to dig deeper.

"Forever Midnight has many businesses. Bars, restaurants. A bike shop or two. Hell, you might even say we're nigh on fucking legit these days," he said while I took a sip from the bottle.

"These days?" I asked.

"Since, the blessed state of Colorado, legalized cannabis cultivation, providing we keep our license up to date." He sighed and turned to me, his face a mask of concentration. "Life can be rough and tumble sometimes, and by that, I mean brothers get shot," he patted the scar by his waist, "or stabbed, and they inflict the fucking same in return. Right now, we have a problem with the Feral Sons. Hell, we always have problems with the Feral Sons. Now those are some bad dudes, they'd piss on their own mothers for a buck. They've been trying to muscle in on our business for years, drive us out of a few towns they think belong to them. They're making a mistake pushing Caleb around. Forever Midnight may be mostly legit these days, but we take care of fucking business when we have to. I know you've had issues with your stepbrother, but the world you come from princess is very different from the one you've found here."

I clutched my stomach and rubbed my arms, pushing down the nausea that threatened to churn my stomach. Cane had put me on some weird pedestal and made a whole world of assumptions about me. I may not cuss every other word or have a body covered in tattoos. I'd been privately educated. I'd even fostered the delusion that one day I'd become a doctor, but I was no princess. Our worlds were not all that different, no matter how much it may look like they were on the outside.

A sobbing breath escaped my lips. Cane walked over and pulled me into his arms. I rested my head on his chest.

How could I tell him that my stepdad was a drug dealer, or rather, a drug baron? Forever Midnight may be nigh on legit, but there was nothing legit about my family business. They may dress fancy and live in a big house with a pool, but a polished turd is still a turd. What was it Mom had said? *'I'm not as precious as I think I am'*. It was worse than that — I closed my eyes and focused on Cane's heartbeat and the movement of his chest — I wasn't as precious as Cane thought I was.

He ran his hand over my chin and lifted my head to look at him. "You okay?" he asked. When I didn't respond, he shifted his head and rubbed at my cheek with his beard, tickling it, until I smiled. "You okay?" he asked again before taking a deep breath. "I think it's time we talked about your brother and what he did to you."

He kissed me on the forehead and pulled away, taking my hand, and walking me back to the chairs by the fireplace. He sat down and pulled me to sit on top of him. He was silent for a few minutes, and I wondered what he was thinking. His neck was corded again, and his body seemed tense. He stroked the side of my face and gently brushed my hair behind my ear.

"Did he rape you?" he asked through gritted teeth.

I shook my head. "His father forbade him until I turned

twenty-one."

Cane cleared his throat. "How old are you now?"

"I turned twenty-one the week before I ran away. That was two months ago."

He squeezed me tighter and ran his hand over my head as though smoothing my hair.

"So, if I'm understanding correctly, that means he now has his father's blessing to rape you."

"I guess it does." I didn't feel the need to add he had my mom's blessing too. None of that mattered. Rape was disgusting and terrifying, and the thought of Daniel touching me in any way made me want to scream. It was obvious Cane thought that was the worst thing Daniel could do to me, but he was wrong.

"I was thirteen, the first time we had one of our *'sessions'* as Daniel likes to call them." I clamped my eyes shut to stop the tears from falling. "He told me to go down to the basement and fetch his philosophy book as he was late for class. I'd lived with him for a year by then and had already learned that all the men who worked for my stepdad did what Daniel said, despite his being much younger than them. I'd automatically done the same. Plus, I'd never been in the basement before. It was off-limits, and I was a little excited to find out what was down there."

"What was down there?" Cane asked.

"No books." I huffed out a breath and wiped the tears from my eyes. I'd never told anyone what happened down there. None of my school friends. Not even my mom, although she knew. It felt weird to be talking about it now, but Cane had asked, and it felt right to share it with him. "There was nothing there. It was dark and dusty and smelled like dirty socks. Only a single chair sat in the middle of the room alongside a small desk with a few things on it. None of them were books."

My heart raced, and I heard its beat echoing back at me from Cane's chest. "Daniel followed me," I said. "He grabbed me from behind before shoving a cloth in my mouth, and then pushed me into the chair."

At the memory, my breaths came fast, and I was in danger of hyperventilating. I tried to move, but when I lifted my hand to push myself up, it was shaking, and all my strength had left me.

Cane clasped onto it with his own hand and pressed my palm to his chest. "It's okay," he said. "He can't find you here."

I wanted to tell him he was wrong, that Daniel would find me anywhere, with or without a tracker. Hell, if he got a good look at Cane back at the bar, he'd have seen the emblem on his jacket and would know everything there was to know about the motorcycle club by now. Even if he hadn't, he knew I'd been working at the bar, and that Cherrie and Greg had been trying to help me. Checking out Forever Midnight would be the first step in locating me.

I was playing a waiting game, knowing what was coming and how futile it was to avoid it. I'd accepted my fate as Mom wanted. I guess you could call the time I'd spent with Cane my last hurrah.

"He bound me to the chair with duct tape and told me I was never to call him D-Dan again." Even now, it was hard to say the word, to let it escape from my lips. "He kneeled before me and pulled the rag from my mouth. I'd sobbed and pleaded with him to untie me. Everyone called him Dan. It was how he'd been introduced. I didn't know any better. From then on, I was only ever to call him Daniel. I agree, said I was sorry, and that it would never happen again. But that wasn't good enough. He said I had to learn. He shoved the rag back in my mouth and taped it in place. Then he put the tape over my nostrils, and stood, never taking his eyes off me. I struggled at first, desperate to break free. Then I stopped."

Even though I sat safely within Cane's arms, I was taken back to all the times Daniel had tied me to the chair. My mind swam. Panic flooded my body as though it was happening all over again. I kept talking, telling Cane what had happened, but my voice felt as though it was coming from a great distance.

"I couldn't find the strength to move," I said. "The room got darker. It shrank in, closer and closer, until all I could see was

Daniel's silhouette in a stark red outline. I knew then I was going to die, but Daniel moved, he ripped the tape from my mouth and pulled out the cloth."

Cold sweat glistened on my brow. I pushed away from Cane and jumped to my feet, gulping in breaths. My hand shook uncontrollably. I couldn't breathe. I had to get air. I had to get out. I rushed to the cabin door, but couldn't open it. My head swam and my vision blurred. I had to get out. The room was too small.

"Thea," Cane said and grabbed each side of my face, keeping it locked on his. "It's okay. You're fine."

"I can't breathe."

Cane opened the door and pulled me with him onto the porch, engulfing me in his arms. "Take a deep breath," he said. I gulped in the fresh forest air as though I'd been drowning. "Good, and another. I've got you. I promise. I will keep you safe forever. I promise."

I looked into his face, at his serious lines, gruff beard, and concerned eyes, and knew he meant what he said. I just wish I believed he was able to.

"He did it three more times in that particular session," I said. "Each time, I felt certain I was about to die."

Cane swallowed and took a deep breath of his own. "How many sessions were there?" he asked.

"Too many to count."

His neck corded, and the vein on his forehead twitched. "Did he... Is that... is that everything?"

"If he wasn't in the mood to watch me die, he would push the chair, so its back rested on the floor and my bare feet, bound to its legs by my ankles, pointed in the air. He'd hit the arches of my feet with a rod until he got bored of my screams."

Cane's muscles tensed, and he felt fit to burst, but his voice was steady and calm when he asked how many times that happened.

"Too many to count," I answered.

CHAPTER TWELVE

Cane

A clamp of icy anger, more cold and deadly than any I'd ever felt before settled over my heart when Thea told me what her stepbrother had done to her.

Bono had talked about things like that happening in Guantanamo Bay. Dry-boarding, I think he'd called it. Fuck, it was bad enough to think the army used the technique to torture detainees, but they were trying to keep the country safe. Doing it to a kid, a thirteen-year-old girl… There's no surprise she's fucked-up. In fact, the big surprise was that she's not as fucked-up as she should be. We should call *her* Lucky, as it was a fucking miracle she's still alive.

I wanted to phone Caleb and see if he'd found out anything about the fucker. It was past time I paid him a visit. But the only thing that mattered at that moment was getting Thea to breathe and getting her to realize that I was there for her and intended to keep her safe.

She'd been so strong and decisive since arriving at my cabin. It was hard to reconcile the fuck-goddess she'd become with the innocent and fragile mess she'd been at the bar and during her ketamine trip. But as soon as she talked about Dan — fuck am I ever calling him Daniel — and what he'd done, that person came swooping back.

I should have kept my fucking questions to myself and spared her the trauma.

He'd done these unbelievable things to her not once, not twice, but too many times to count. I wanted to know more, if there was anything else, he'd done to her. I wanted to do the exact same things to him, but Thea couldn't take any more of my questions. Instead, I lifted her in my arms and carried her upstairs to bed. She lay against my chest, silently crying until all the emotion tired her out and she fell asleep.

Hell, five hours before we'd lay in the exact same spot and the only thing on my mind was how quickly I could be inside her again. Now, I rested in shocked silence, wanting nothing more than to take all her pain away and remove its cause.

"Fuck, Caleb," I said as I looked at her perfect face and the eyelashes that kissed her soft cheeks. "You were right, after all. I do have it bad."

Eventually, sleep claimed me too. Only when my phone rang

downstairs did I stir. Thea was still resting against my chest, and I had a crook in my neck from the odd position I'd slept in against the headboard.

She lifted her head and rested her chin on my chest, huffing a breath into my beard. "Morning," she said and flashed me a smile. Her way, I guessed, of letting me know she was okay now and not about to have another breakdown.

"Morning," I said, echoing her words. My way of reassuring her I was calm enough not to rip anyone's fucking head off. At least on the outside.

She pushed herself up and glanced down the stairs, where my phone still rang. "You'd better get that."

"Nah. They can ring back."

They did, three seconds after the first call rang off. Knowing it had to be Caleb, and he'd likely send Bono over to smash down my door if I didn't answer this time, I slid from the bed and slipped down the stairs.

"What you got on this fucker, Caleb?" I asked, wanting to get straight to the point.

"Nothing good," was all he said in reply. "Look, I need you to get down to the clubhouse, like now. And I'm not fucking kidding. I need you out of that door within the next two minutes."

The tone in his voice was urgent and I worried that things

had kicked off with the Feral Sons. I sat on the chair at the table and rested my head in my hands. "I can't leave Thea, and I don't want to risk bringing her into town."

"Fucking leave her," he said.

"I just said, I can't *fucking* leave her. If any shit's that urgent, you can tell me over the phone." I couldn't keep the anger and frustration out of my voice and didn't want to. It was about fucking time Caleb accepted that Thea was now part of my life, even if I was still figuring out what part that might be.

Caleb huffed a breath down the line and fell silent. I waited for him to spit out whatever the hell he had to say next. A hand rested on my shoulder. I jumped from the chair, but this time, I controlled my urge to lash out and punch my assailant in the face.

"Fuck, woman! How the hell do you move so quietly?"

Her face dipped to the floor, and she clutched her stomach, rubbing at her arm. I instantly regretted the question. The answer was obvious: years and years of practice; years and years of trying to stay unnoticed, so Dan-the-Motherfucker wouldn't hear her and decide it was time for another '*session*'.

"I'm sorry," I said. "Just try and give me a warning before you get too close in the future. Clear your throat or call my name or something. Hell, throw a fucking brick at my head… just let me know when you're coming, okay? I'd hate to accidentally punch you on reflex."

A mischievous smile played at the edge of her lips as she raised her head from the ground. She'd foregone my T-shirt this time and wore nothing but her black bra and panties. "A brick, you say. You sure it won't bounce off that thick head unnoticed?"

And just like that, my fuck-goddess was back, and my cock sprang to attention in my sweatpants. From anyone else, the words would be offensive, but from Thea, they were a come-on.

"I'll show you a thick head."

"Promises. Promises." Her eyes flicked to the phone, forgotten in my hand. "Shouldn't you finish your call first?"

"Shit!" I lifted the phone to my ear. "Caleb, you still there?"

"Where the *fuck* else am I gonna be? ... Look," he said, his voice flat. "I realize you've got a new toy to play with, but she can wait. I need you here, twenty minutes ago."

I rubbed at my head, wanting to smash his face in for calling Thea a toy. Just because he'd gotten fucked-up over a girl who left him and had brushed aside all notions of a meaningful relationship, didn't mean I had to. "We're going around in circles here. I'm not leaving. Now. Speak. Carefully. Brother."

Caleb grumbled but didn't comment on my tone. "I gave Bono a quick call on the other line while you two were having your little *tete-a-tete*, or whatever the fuck you want to call it. Unlike you, he listens to me and does what I ask. He'll be with your *lady friend* in a little over fifteen minutes."

"If Bono's here in fifteen minutes and Thea's comfortable with his presence, then, and only then, will I leave."

Thea cleared her throat and touched my arm. "You should go," she said.

"What? No fucking way. I'm not leaving you here alone."

"I won't be alone." She shifted nervously on the spot. "Bono's the one who gave me Advil, right? The one with the marine tattoo?" I nodded and she huffed out a breath. "Then, I'll be fine. I'll lock myself in the bathroom until I hear a motorcycle outside."

"You're not gonna fucking lock yourself in the bathroom. This is stupid. I'll wait until Bono gets here and then I'll go."

"Please," she said and trailed her fingers down my arm before squeezing my hand. "I'll be fine. Don't let me be a source of problems between you and your brother. I've already caused you enough bother."

I mumbled a cuss under my breath and my mind went numb. I didn't want to leave, but the look on her face told me I was causing her more pain by staying.

Fuck! Fuck! Fuck!

"Are you a hundred-fucking-percent sure?" I asked.

"I am. If Daniel knew where I was, he'd be here already. I'll be fine by myself until Bono arrives and then fine with him until you get back."

My shoulders slumped. Her mind was made up, and I didn't want to add to her problems and have her worrying that she was the source of any trouble between me and Caleb. I sighed and lifted my phone to my ear. "You hear that?" I asked.

"I did."

"You got anything to say about it?"

Caleb shifted on the other end of the line. For a second, I wondered if he was going to change his mind and tell me to stay. Instead, he mumbled out a two-word answer before hanging up the phone: "Leave now."

I dropped my phone on the table and pulled Thea into my arms, kissing her gently on the forehead. Then I whipped her up the stairs and told her to get dressed, while I did the same.

We got our clothes on in record time, and I positioned her by the window. "Don't lock yourself in the bathroom," I said. "Stand right here and keep your eye on the road. If you see any fucker beside one of my brothers in a Forever Midnight MC jacket, then you get your ass out the back door. There's a trail that leads to the forest. Follow it, hide, and I'll come for you. Don't come out of hiding until you hear my voice. You got it?"

Her brow furrowed and her eyes flashed to the back door, looking for all the world like she was noticing it for the first time. "It's a little overkill, but I've got it. Now, go. You're making me nervous."

"I'm keeping you safe. If you need anything, tell Bono to call me straight away. I'll call you as soon as I reach the clubhouse, which will be in about 40 minutes, okay?"

Without giving her the chance to answer, I kissed her one final time and grabbed my keys and phone before rushing out the door. I hopped on my bike and turned on the engine, but hesitated and glanced back to the cabin.

This better be fucking important, Caleb!

Thea waved and I nodded before pulling away.

CHAPTER THIRTEEN

Thea

I stood, staring out the window, unable to contain the rolling in my stomach that appeared as Cane rode out of view. I held my breath, listening until the last rumble of his bike faded from my ears. But then, I was too afraid to gasp in air in case I missed the sound of Bono's arrival.

I felt more alone in this little cabin in the woods than I ever had, and couldn't help but think, out here, no one would hear me scream. Not that anyone ever came to help when I did back home.

The forest was too noisy. Every rustle of leaves in the wind or squawk of a bird pierced my eardrums and made me wince. Why couldn't they just shut up? I strained harder waiting for the sound of Bono's bike to reach my senses, but it never came. I sat down on the ground, tired of standing, and clasped onto the window ledge. After a while, I moved my gaze from the gravel road that wound through the dense forest with its tangled branches and creeping vines and stared at the hardwood floor.

I closed my eyes and huffed out a breath before shaking my head and giving a wry laugh.

"Get a grip, Thea," I told myself, making sure to say the words out loud to break the silence stifling the air.

I stood, ran my hands over my stomach before resting them on my hips, and took a few deep breaths. I had no way to tell the time, and even though it seemed an eternity since Cane left, it could very well have been only a few minutes.

Not wanting to torment myself with staring out the window, I decided my best bet would be to check out the path that Cane had mentioned led into the forest. I wouldn't go far and could come back to the cabin as soon as I heard Bono arrive.

I opened the back door and sucked in the forest air. A bird zipped overhead, making me duck, and then laugh. If I ever wanted a normal life with Cane, I had to stop jumping at the slightest sound. I'd drive him away if I was too clingy and stifled his freedom. Although — I shook my head — was that what I wanted? To stay with Cane. Even if I did, and it was possible, there was no saying Cane wanted it to either.

The morning sun cast a golden sheen over the trees and mountains, and the woody incense of fir and pine wafted on the breeze as I walked up the path. The beckoning forest seemed safer than it had when I'd first arrived, and I wondered what had changed. Something inside me was different. I felt an overwhelming certainty that had to do with Cane.

Maybe having someone want to take care of me instead of feeding me to the dogs had made me place value on myself. "Hell, Mom," I said, wanting to stick my fingers up at her. "Maybe I am precious, after all."

The memory of her following me out of the kitchen with a bottle of red wine in her hand surfaced. *'It's better to accept your fate.'* Her words echoed in my mind, and I felt like my head was spinning. Once again, the cold hard certainty that Daniel would find me settled around my heart.

What was it Cane's dad had said about midnight? How a sense of peace came over the world and he wished he could stay in that moment forever. As I trudged along the path leading to the forest, I knew that was what I'd been doing. I'd been living in one forever-moment with Cane, and sooner or later the spell would be broken. The tear winding down my cheek told me that maybe, it just had.

I shouldn't be here when Cane returned. It would be easier for both of us if I just disappeared.

A strange urge to run through the forest surfaced. I needed to feel the wind on my face and experience a final rush of freedom that could only come from knowing that no one was around to watch me fall.

Before I could take my first step, the skin on the back of my neck crawled and my every instinct turned to high alert. My initial thought was that Bono had arrived, or better yet, Cane had returned, but that was the voice of hope and not reality.

I turned to look at the cabin. I'd left the back door open. The inside was dark, and no trace of movement met my gaze. I scanned the small clearing and the surrounding forest. There were no cars or bikes visible, but from my position, the cabin blocked my view of the main parking area. The only creatures that greeted me were the birds and the chirping grasshoppers.

The hot August sun beat down on my head and body, causing my skin to tingle from its warm caress, but goosebumps prickled my arms and I found it hard to shake the feeling of danger.

I stood frozen to the spot, halfway between the cabin and the concealment of the woods, not knowing what to do and worried that any movement on my part would draw attention. If there was attention to be drawn.

Feeling silly, and as though my imagination was kicking into overdrive again, I considered calling out to Bono, but something froze my tongue.

Damn it!

Deep down, I knew that eventually, Daniel would find me,

but did that knowledge have me jumping at non-existent ghosts in the forest?

One thing was certain, I had to move. I'd run to the forest and circle around to the cabin we'd passed on the way in. Maybe they had a phone, and I could call a cab. After that, I'd be out of Cane's hair forever. Even if the thought of never seeing him again did cause a lump in my throat and a heaviness in my chest. It was for the best. Daniel wouldn't think twice about having one of Tony's men put a bullet in his head. Hell, he might even expend the effort and do it himself. I could always phone the bar and leave a message with Cherrie, just so Cane knew I was safe, and he wasn't to come looking for me.

I turned my back to the cabin and picked up my speed, focusing on my destination. The grassy hill led up to the sun-kissed treetops beyond. I made my way to the woods, my breath tight in my throat.

When I reached the tree line, I gave my surroundings a final scan and saw nothing. "Goodbye, Cane," I said to his cabin. "It was fun while it lasted."

Without another word, I stepped into the forest and broke into a run. Not an easy thing to do with all the branches and roots underfoot. My pulse quickened and my breath came in shallow gasps, but the wind brushed my hair from my face and allowed me to breathe again.

I almost jumped when a faint breeze rustled through the thicket, and a mouse shuffled through the undergrowth to my left. I laughed at my jitteriness, but worried that next time it might be a mountain lion or worse.

I ran on, twisting in the direction I knew would lead me to the cabin we'd passed on the way to Cane's. The scent of sweet, summer berries filled the air and me with a fresh sense of purpose. I was doing the right thing.

The tread of footsteps thudded behind me.

I had a fraction of a second to turn my head before a man easily twice my size plowed into me and sent me careening into the rough bark of a tree, grazing my cheek.

The form was too large to be Daniel, and Cane would never jump me in the forest.

Despite the dizziness that threatened to overwhelm me, I lashed out with my leg and landed a satisfying kick on my attacker's. Adrenaline rushed through my veins. I jumped up and faced the man before me.

I was right. It wasn't Daniel, but my legs shook, and I almost fell again when I realized it was one of the men who worked for my stepfather.

"Jacob," I said, amazed at my ability to find my voice. "Please, just let me go. Tell Tony you couldn't find me. Please, you can't take me back."

A menacing smile filled his face. "It's funny how you think you can ask a favor of me, bitch. Do you think I've forgotten all the times you looked down your snotty little nose at me?"

"I-I never. I was just..." How could I say I was too afraid of anyone who came into the house to look them in the face?

"You were a fucking tease. Like I didn't hear you've been shacked up with some biker. You play that butter wouldn't melt in your mouth crap with him?"

My heart nosedived into my stomach. Mom had called me a cock-tease, too. What the hell did everyone think of me? That I'd been playing some silly game with them my whole life?

"Tony tasked me with bringing you home, and that's what I'm gonna do. Although, interestingly enough, after Danny-boy heard where you've been the past few days, he's not too bothered about the condition you're in when you get there."

I stood frozen to the ground, unable to do anything but watch as Jacob slipped his hands to his waistband and unfastened his belt. The buckle shimmered in the light as he doubled over the leather, held it in one hand, and slapped it over the palm of the other.

He swung it at my head, and I fell to the ground, raising my hands to protect me. It was the searing crack I heard as the leather hit my forearm, more than I felt the pain itself. At least, at first.

I screamed. My arm felt as though it was on fire.

Jacob grabbed my hair and yanked my head back. "It's about time you were on your knees before me."

The stench of his breath filled my nostrils and a glob of spit landed on my face. I clawed at his hand, to free it from my hair. When that failed, I beat at his arms and shoulders. Bile rose in my throat.

Jacob laughed and threw me to the ground. I flipped over onto my front, and dug into the ground, pulling myself along, desperate to get away. He grabbed hold of my leg and pulled me towards him, flipping me on my back before straddling my legs.

He threw the belt to the side, and pushed his hand up my top, squeezing my breast tightly. I cried out and tried to push him away, but he was too strong.

"I can't breathe. Please, I can't breathe." The words came out in rasping breaths, barely audible above the pulse thrashing in my ears. I was suffocating. His weight was too much. The forest was closing in.

Jacob's hand slid over my stomach and fumbled with the buttons on my jeans. I filled my lungs with as much air as I could. I screamed and screamed again while tears ran down my cheeks.

His heavy hand grasped my throat and squeezed. "Shut the fuck up or I'll make sure you can't breathe." He loosened his grip and I gasped for air.

Fear that he'd do it again washed all the fight from my body. My eyes glazed over and I stiffened, trying to imagine myself anywhere but here.

CHAPTER FOURTEEN

Cane

I thought the worst when the phone vibrated in my pocket. All moisture fled my mouth and a pang hit deep in my stomach.

"Bono," I said as soon as I'd pulled the bike over to the side of the road and answered the call. I was on the outside of town and had another few miles to go before I reached the clubhouse. "Is Thea okay?"

"That's what I was calling to ask you."

My fists tightened and my neck corded. If Thea wasn't at the cabin, then something bad must have happened. It was easily half an hour since I'd left. My anger surged along with my worry. "Why the fuck did it take you so long to get to my cabin?"

"Cane. Calm down a second. I'm not at your cabin. I have no idea what you're talking about."

My temperature spiked, but an icy dread pierced my heart.

I wanted to pick my bike up and throw it at Caleb's head. The fucker had lied.

"Caleb didn't call you earlier and ask you to head over to my place and take care of Thea, did he?" I asked to be certain. The silence that greeted me was answer enough. "I'm gonna kill him."

"Calm down," Bono said again. As if telling anyone to calm down ever had anything but the opposite fucking effect. "If Caleb lied to you, we both know there has to be a good reason."

"We both know he couldn't give a flying fuck for Thea's mental state or wellbeing." I glanced back up the road I'd come along. A few cars zipped by. One honked their horn and gestured as though pissed off I was staring. At this time of day, traffic had been heavy, but I'd made sure to glance in every car that passed to see if Dan was driving. But I couldn't check vehicles coming in from the opposite direction. "I need you to get to my cabin as soon as possible. Thea's likely in a panic by now. She was expecting you almost twenty minutes ago."

"Will do. Where are you?"

"Just outside of town. I was on the way to the clubhouse."

"Then, you'll likely beat me to it. I'm with Rex. We were at his place going through all the CCTV he collected the other night."

"Fuck! I gotta go."

~

I didn't think I could feel worse than I had when Bono called, but as I rounded the bend before my cabin and saw a black fucking SUV parked outside, my vision closed in around me and I couldn't focus on anything else but that motherfucking car.

The front door to the cabin was open. Through it, I noted the back door was open too.

Good girl. She must have run and hidden, just like I told her.

Without caring what damage it would do to my bike, or how much it would rattle my brain, I circled around back and took the Harley off-road and up the hill to the forest. The suspension sure as hell wasn't built for the dirt path, but its torque and low center of gravity worked to my advantage, and it was a damn sight better than me trying to run up the hill.

As soon as I reached the top, I flung the bike to the side and entered the forest. Now, all I had to do was find Thea before any fucker else did.

I edged deeper beneath the canopy, listening for the faintest sound, but the only noise was my own fucking breath, hissing in and out like a goddamn snake. I trod lightly, being careful not to make any more sound. With each step, my worry grew, and when a heart-breaking scream ripped through the air, I felt as though my soul had been torn in two.

I was a fucking idiot to leave her. I'd promised to keep her safe and failed.

I charged in the direction of the sound. Another scream came a few minutes later, then another. The sound choked off, and I nearly fell to my knees and wept at the silence that followed. Only knowing Thea needed me kept my feet moving.

A flicker of movement caught my gaze through the trees. I increased my pace, and as I got closer and saw some fucker tugging on Thea's jeans with one hand while the other was wrapped around her throat, a guttural roar bubbled up from my chest and escaped my lips. I charged. The pounding of my steps matched the thumping of my heart, and my nostrils flared.

I barreled into the fucker, driving him from Thea's body, and showed no mercy as I pummeled my fists into his face. He lifted his hands to protect himself, but I batted them away. In a strength only found in pure rage, I lifted him by the neck and held him in place against a tree while I continued to smash my fist into his head. Only when the metallic scent of blood filled my senses, and I was satisfied the fucker would never move, let alone lay a finger on Thea again, did I stop.

I dropped him to the floor, wiped the blood from my hands and face in his shirt, and then turned to Thea.

She stood frozen in place with a mixture of relief and shock on her face. I reached out and pulled her into a deep embrace. "Are you okay?" I asked when all I wanted to do was beg for her forgiveness.

"He... he worked for my stepdad. H-he was..."

"I know. But he didn't. Let me look at you." I pulled back.

Her face was grazed with a gash on the side, the makings of fingertip bruises mottled the skin of her neck, and she held her arm strangely. She winced and hissed out a breath when I took a hold of it to get a better view. An angry welt ran along her forearm. On top of that, one of the fingernails was ripped from its bed, and all were covered in mud as though she'd clawed at the ground.

If I hadn't already killed the fucker, I'd do it again.

I brushed her hair out of her face and pulled her in for another hug. "He might not have been alone," I said as I glanced around the forest, peering into their depths. "We have to get out of here."

I cleared my throat and took a deep breath before pulling back, though it was the last thing I wanted to do. I felt an emptiness inside without Thea in my arms, as though I was deserting her all over again, but we had to move.

"You found me," she said. "How did you know?"

"We need to go."

Thea glanced from me to her attacker and back again. "I don't understand. How did this happen? How did you know to come back?" A questioning look filled her eyes, and I knew she sensed I was hiding something.

I pulled her in for another hug. "I'm so fucking sorry this is happening. I'll tell you everything when we get somewhere safe."

"Somewhere safe?" Thea glanced around the forest and shuddered. "There is nowhere safe."

I gripped her shaking hands. I wanted to tell her she was wrong, but how could I when I suspected my own brother had known this man was on his way to Thea when he told me to leave? When I suspected he'd given away her location in the first place.

"Can you walk?" I asked, instead.

Thea nodded. I held her hand and half dragged her through the forest, keeping a swift pace as I steered us towards Bono's place.

As soon as we were out of view of the body, I sat Thea next to a tree and told her I had to make a phone call. When she didn't let go of my hand, I brushed her hair behind her ear and kissed her on the forehead. "I'm going to be no more than ten steps in that direction," I said and pointed to a spot a little ahead of where we'd stopped. "You'll be able to see me the whole time, okay?"

Thea nodded and released my hand, but her eyes burned with questions.

I pulled my phone from my pocket and dialed Bono's

number. He didn't answer, so I hung up and tried again. After I hung up for the second time, the phone rang in my hand.

"Bono, where are you?" I asked.

"About ten minutes away. I had to pull over to take the call."

I ran my hand through my hair and searched the shadows of the forest for any sign of life. "I need you to turn back and go to the clubhouse," I said. "I also need to borrow your Jeep."

"What's going on?" Bono asked.

I glanced at Thea and gave her a smile before turning my back and lowering my voice. "I need to know what the fuck Caleb is playing at." I gave Bono a quick run-down of what I'd found when I'd returned, and my suspicion that Celeb was involved in telling Thea's stepdad her location. "Just go to the clubhouse and tell him, Thea is safe with me, and I intend to keep her that way. Find out why he fucking did what he did."

"You don't know for definite he's involved," Bono said, but I huffed out a breath. I knew.

"Just do it for me, will you? I'll call you when we're on the road."

"Make sure you do. Stay safe, brother."

"I intend to." With that, I ended the call, moved back to Thea, and kneeled on the ground before her.

"How are you holding up?" I asked.

Thea closed her eyes and let out a deep breath before

opening them again. "I'm cold and really hungry, but I'm okay."

The midday sun beat down on the trees overhead and sent a spattering of rays through their branches. It was cool amongst the trees, but it was anything but cold.

"It's the shock," I said, taking off my jacket and wrapping it around her shoulders. She slid her arms in place, and I pulled her to her feet. "You need to try and relax," I added. "You're wound up tighter than a fucking jack-in-the-box fit to explode."

I cleared my throat and ran my hand over my beard when she gave me a look that screamed, how the hell was that gonna happen? I'd be damned if I knew.

Fuck! This time yesterday had been perfect. Thea and I had fucked all day long without a care in the world, or at least we pretended so at the time. But then, I'd deserted her, left her vulnerable when I'd promised to keep her safe. And then there was that fucker from the SUV.

An image of what might have happened if I hadn't found her bombarded my mind. There was no fucking way he wouldn't have raped her, and fuck knew what else. The why of it made no sense to me. What? Thea had turned twenty-one, so she wasn't just fair game for Dan, but all her fucking stepdad's employees on top? No wonder Dan was a sick fuck, his dad was too.

I tensed and growled. Thea may be wound tighter than a jack-in-the-box fit to explode, but I was angrier than a puffed toad.

"We'd better get moving," I said, taking her hand and focusing my mind on getting to Bono's without falling and breaking our legs on the bracken-laced undergrowth. "We'll see what food he has and get cleaned up when we get there."

Thea didn't speak, but she squeezed my hand and rested her head on my arm for a few seconds, before stepping ahead and pulling me behind her.

CHAPTER FIFTEEN

Thea

I tried to focus on the birds singing and the wind whistling through the branches. Cane might not realize it, but this forest was our last haven of safety and calm. The last time, we could pretend the outside world didn't exist.

He'd made a mistake killing Jacob. My emotions warred with themselves. They flicked from being glad that he had to wishing he hadn't and being concerned about what would happen next. Tony wasn't sadistic like Daniel. He didn't get off on watching people suffer, but he didn't think twice about killing people when they messed with him or got in the way of his business. Jacob had worked for Tony for over twenty years. To say my stepfather would not be pleased when he found out he was dead was an understatement.

Despite what happened, and my growing hunger, I could have stayed beneath the dappled shade of the trees forever. I imagined Cane's arms around me, and my head on his chest; his warmth seeping into me. We could stay that way all day and watch the streams of light fade beneath the canopy. Waiting until the sun sank lower in the sky, drifting below the horizon. We could have one final forever-midnight: one final moment of peace.

My stomach grumbled, breaking our silence. A fly flew too close to my face and made my nose twitch.

Cane squeezed my hand. "Only another fifteen minutes' walk until we reach Bono's."

I sighed, wishing it was longer. But I also knew that no matter how hungry I was, Cane had to be worse. Neither of us had eaten anything since the pizza last night, and he needed a lot more calories than I did to keep him going.

"There's something you need to know," I said and glanced to the east, searching for the sun. It had moved almost overhead, and I guessed that meant we were nearing midday. I sucked in a breath. The forest reeked of age and permanence, as though life would always be here, never changing, but ever-growing, and ever-teeming with creatures untouched by the concerns of the human world. I cleared my throat and continued, "My stepfather is Tony Benton. He's a…"

I was about to say more when Cane stopped in his tracks and turned to stare at me. The look in his eyes hardened, and

I knew he'd heard the name before. "I thought you said your stepbrother's surname was King."

I fidgeted on the spot, unable to look him in the eye. "It is. Daniel's mother died when he was two. When he was sixteen, he took on her maiden name to honor her memory." He also wanted to make a name for himself and not fall under the shadow of his father's.

"*Fuck!*" He rubbed at his beard and brushed his hands through his hair, grabbing onto the top of his head. "*Fuck,*" he said again.

I reached towards him, but stopped when I saw the look on his face, and clutched my belly instead. "I'm sorry," I said, unable to keep the hitch from my voice.

Cane turned his face to the sky, and a well of emptiness filled my insides. After a moment that stretched for far too long, he cleared his throat and nodded his head as though resigned to something.

"It doesn't matter," he said and reached for my hand again. "It changes nothing. I'd have done exactly what I have regardless."

He was wrong. If he'd known who my father was when we first met, he would never have destroyed the tracker. Hell, if Cherrie and Greg had known who I was, they would never have taken me in.

"We should get to Bono's," I said.

Cane nodded, but we'd only taken two steps before he stopped again. "That's why Caleb told him where you fucking were! It doesn't excuse the fucker, but at least I can understand a little of his reason why."

My brows furrowed, and I rubbed at my eyes. "Oh, God," I said and rested my face in my hands. All traces of hunger vanished from my body as my appetite left me. When I stood tall again and looked at Cane, I could tell he thought I was shocked by his brother's actions and hadn't realized that things had just gotten a lot worse. Though it was hard to imagine such a thing was possible "Tony is going to think your brother betrayed him. Jacob's dead, and Tony will lay that blame on every single member of the Forever Midnight Motorcycle Club."

Cane's neck corded and the vein in his temple throbbed as my words sank in. "Fuck," he said again before grabbing my hand and pulling me through the forest at a faster pace.

"You should call him and warn him," I said.

"I will. At Bono's. I just have to figure out what I'm gonna fucking say first."

At the pace we were moving, it took less than ten minutes to arrive at Bono's cabin. It took Cane a few minutes after that to retrieve the spare key from under the porch. When he finally opened the door, the hum of an air-conditioning unit greeted me as I stepped through. I shivered in the blast of cold air.

On the outside, Bono's cabin was much the same as Cane's: a simple one-story log cabin with steps leading up to a front porch and a converted roof space, but inside was a lot cozier. Besides the addition of the AC unit, Bono also had a TV, two sofas, and a coffee table.

Cane went straight into one of the cupboards and pulled out a first-aid kit.

"We should eat first." I headed to the kitchen area and noted a loaf of bread on the counter. "A sandwich will be quick."

"We should clean you up first." He grabbed my hand and lifted it to my face. Beneath the caked mud, I noticed one of my nails had come completely off. It must have happened when I'd been clawing into the ground to try and drag myself away from Jacob. I'd noted a throbbing pain in my hand, but assumed I'd just bruised it. With my hand still in his, Cane walked me over to the sink and turned on the tap. "This is gonna hurt."

I winced when the water hit my hands, but stayed still while Cane cleared the mud from them. Afterward, he dried them with the towel, and then wet the corner of it to dab at my face. This time, I let out a hiss. After he finished, Cane sprayed my finger with antiseptic wound spray and bandaged it up, before opting for just the spray on my face.

Throughout it all, his face was a mask of concentration and

his entire body tense, but he never looked into my eyes. As soon as he'd finished, he went straight to the fridge and pulled out some ham and cheese, slamming it on the counter before grabbing the bread. When he looked more like he would throw it against the wall than make a sandwich, I took it from his hands and grabbed the butter from the fridge.

"What are you thinking?" I asked when Cane paced the room.

"I'm wondering how the hell we're gonna get out of this." He ran his hand through his hair, and perched on the edge of the sofa, shaking his head.

The answer was easy, but I wasn't about to tell him. I had to go back. I had to tell Tony that Jacob tried to rape me, and in a fit of rage, I smashed him in the face with a stone and didn't stop. Hell, if Tony decided to kill me, it would be a blessing. But it was more likely he'd hand me over to Daniel. I just had to get away from Cane before I could do it.

I finished making the sandwiches and we sat in silence while we ate. After we'd finished, I took the plates and cleaned up.

"Maybe you should take a shower before we leave." I eyed the blood splatter on his top.

Cane followed my gaze, before whipping his T-shirt off. "You go first," he said. "There's no telling when we'll get the chance to again."

Sensing that was a dismissal, I bowed my head, and because the layout of the cabin was the same as Cane's, headed to where I knew I'd find the bathroom.

Only after I'd stripped off my clothes and felt the warm water hit my skin did I allow myself to cry.

CHAPTER SIXTEEN

Cane

As soon as Thea shut the bathroom door, I headed outside to call Caleb. Bono might not have reached him yet, although he'd likely guessed I wasn't coming. I was furious with the fucker, and just picturing his face made me want to punch it, but he needed to know what had happened. Maybe he could see if damage control was possible.

He answered the phone within two rings. "Where the fuck are you?" he asked.

I closed my eyes and took a deep breath to calm myself before responding. When I finally felt able to speak, I said, "Thea's stepdad is Tony Benton, but you knew that already. You called me in as you wanted me out of the way when he sent someone to collect her. Someone you told where she was."

My voice strained on the last words. So help me, I could understand his fucking reasoning, but I couldn't forgive it. Not yet. Not when all I could think was what would have happened if Bono had never made that call.

"Where the fuck are you?" he asked again. "I'm not gonna be pleased if you've messed this up."

"Yeah, well, I wasn't fucking pleased to find some motherfucker straddling Thea with one hand on her throat and the other pulling her pants down."

The line went quiet for a few minutes before Caleb asked, "Is he still alive?"

"What the fuck do you think?"

"Shit, Cane. Do you have any idea what you've done? And for what, some spoiled princess who—"

"This is on you, not me." I paced the deck, unable to keep still, unable to listen to this shit. "You sent that fucker to my house."

"Damn right, I did, and if you were thinking with your head instead of your cock, you would see it was the right thing to do." He huffed out a breath before adding, "Benton agreed the girl wouldn't be hurt."

"Yeah, well, big fucking surprise, he lied."

"You need to bring that girl into town. I'll call Benton and arrange another pick-up. Maybe we can salvage something out of this shit-storm you've created."

I laughed. There was a bitter edge to the sound. "I am not

taking Thea anywhere near her family."

"I'm not asking, Cane. I'm telling—"

"No. I'm telling you. It's not gonna fucking happen." With that, I ended the call and let out a string of curses before making another to Bono. It went straight through to voicemail, so I left a message and headed inside.

When I reached the bathroom door, I took a deep breath and rested my forehead on the wood, trying to calm my thoughts before talking to Thea. As soon as I did, the door opened, and I had to reach out and grab the frame to stop myself from falling forward onto her. A small squeak escaped her lips as she took a step back.

She had a towel wrapped around her and held her clothes in her hand. Her cheeks were ruddy, and the graze stood out angry and red against her skin. "I um… I thought it would be quicker if I dressed out here while you showered." When I didn't answer, she clung to her towel and pushed past me into the room.

Not knowing how to put my thoughts into words, I entered the bathroom, closed the door, and turned the shower back on. Then, I leaned on my hands against the sink and looked at myself in the misted mirror.

"What the fuck are you going to do?" I said and shook my head.

I'd always relied on my brothers for back-up, but with Caleb acting the way he was, I couldn't turn to them for help, couldn't risk dragging them in deeper and getting them killed. I'd called Bono and left a message for him to meet us, but beyond that, I didn't know what to do.

With one final glance at my reflection, I pushed away from the unit and flung the door open. Thea had only gone a few steps. I pulled her into my arms and rested her head against my chest. Having her so close sent shivers of need through my body and straight to my cock.

"I'm sorry," Thea said and released a sobbing breath. "I know you're mad at me, but I—"

"Oh, sweetheart. I'm not mad at you." I said, despite the touch of exasperation that leaked into my voice. "I'm just trying to figure out what to do and where we can go that will keep you safe."

Thea lifted her head and gave me a wry smile. She put two fingers on my lips to keep me from talking. Her closeness and delicious scent became too much for me to bear. It felt as though I'd known her for years. I couldn't picture my life without Thea in it. Her whole presence lit up the room and made my day brighter, and when she laughed, I wanted to bury myself deep inside her. Hell, every fucking second, I wanted to bury myself inside her. Fuck me if my heart didn't need her as much as my cock.

An explosion of sensation shot through me as our mouths met and our tongues tangled. Thea bit my lip softly. I was about to relieve her of her towel when I realized something was wrong. Different. This felt like Goodbye.

I pulled back and scowled. "What are you not telling me?" I asked.

Thea's gaze dropped to the floor, and she took a step back, clutching her stomach. But the resolve on her face couldn't be plainer to see. Fuck! She was gonna make a run for it again. As soon as she could, she'd be gone. "There's nothing," she said.

On impulse, I reached out and grasped her hand. "Promise me, you're not gonna run away again."

Thea lifted her head and stared at me with those wide, green eyes. "I'm not gonna run away again," she said. My world shattered as I took in the meaning of her words.

"You are not fucking going back." Anger burned through me at this whole fucked-up situation, cutting the air around us. I pulled her close. "Don't you even think about it."

She yanked her hand from my grasp and pulled away. "It's not your decision to make." The venom in her words reverberated around the room. "It's the only sensible option. Your brother knew it, that's why he told Tony where I was. Why is it so difficult for you to understand?"

Her words slammed into my gut like a runaway freight

train. My fists clenched and my neck corded. Thea took another step back.

Hell, it was time I grew a fucking pair. And stopped acting like a fucking pussy over this woman. After everything she'd been through, she wanted to go back to that fucker. What? Was this all just a game to her? My anger grew.

"I just killed a fucker for you?" I pointed wildly out the window and up into the forests. "Would you have preferred I let him rape you?"

Her hand flew to her mouth to stifle a sob, and a rush of remorse hit me, but left when she said that it might have been better if I had. She grabbed her clothes that had fallen to the floor and took them over to the sofa, perching on its edge. All color drained from her face and her hands were shaking as she tried to put on her jeans.

My anger drained away. She was battered and bruised, and sure as hell didn't need any extra shit from me. I rushed toward her and knelt by her feet. I stilled her hands, and she crumbled against my chest with a tear-stained face. Closing my eyes, I ran my hand over her wet hair and kissed her forehead before pulling back and looking at her. All the heartache and pain in her eyes slapped me across the face.

"This isn't your fault," I said.

"Yes, it is."

I tilted her chin up until she looked at me. "No. It isn't. Caleb fucked up in talking to your stepdad, and I killed the guy in the forest."

"For me."

"For both of us."

Tears streamed down her face again, and without knowing what else to do or say, I pulled her tight against my chest and held her. The only things I knew for certain were that I was never leaving her alone again, and that we had to get on the road as soon as possible. Her stepdad would send someone to find out what was going on soon, and we didn't want to be in the area when that happened.

CHAPTER SEVENTEEN

Thea

I stared out the window of Bono's Jeep and at the river stretched beneath the quiet road bridge. Gentle waves glinted in the afternoon sun, flowing along with the current and lapping at the bank with a tumbling burble. The fresh scent of wet earth cleared the ache that had been building in my head, but did little to still the unease in my stomach.

At Bono's cabin, I'd cried in Cane's arms for an eternity. No matter what I did, the tears wouldn't stop falling. Eventually, Cane lifted my head and said we had to go. When I opened my eyes to look at him and respond, rays of sunlight cracked through the curtains, and I had to blink to clear my vision. Cane's face was a mask of concern.

"You still need to shower," I said.

A smile played at the edge of his lips. "Do I smell that bad?"

He planted me by the door where he said he could keep an

eye on me before stepping into the shower. The water ran over his bare chest, which heaved with every breath. His hand worked the soap over his body, trailing down to rest on his stomach and drawing my attention to his well-defined six-pack, and his massive cock beneath. I swallowed, itching to touch him. To have a repeat of the last shower we had together. I stood, licking my lips, practically drooling at the thought of finally tasting him. Everything about him was achingly beautiful. From his chiseled body to the lines that etched his face.

Every part of me wanted to stay with him forever. But how could I when I'd bring him nothing but danger? Leaving would be hard enough now. How much worse would it be if I allowed myself to love him?

As if he'd sensed my thoughts, Cane turned off the water and lifted the towel to pat his face dry. I could lose myself looking into the deep, brown depths of his eyes. I wanted to reach out and say I was sorry again, to tell him I'd never go. I wanted to pull him close, touch him, and run my fingers through his hair, tangle them in his beard. I wanted to feel him inside me.

His phone rang as he dressed, and he jumped to answer it. Minutes later, we were in the car and headed for a rendezvous with Bono a hundred miles down the road.

Cane talked for almost the entire journey, making plans, and telling me how everything would be okay, but his eyes stayed firmly locked on the road ahead, and I felt like there was something beneath the words he wasn't telling me. My stomach was rumbling by the time we pulled off the highway and into town. The streets were busy until we drove to the large parking lot of a nightclub, deserted during the daytime hours, apart from the four bikes parked close to the doors.

"Another business the brothers own?" I asked while stifling a groan at the name *Club Tempest* sign posted above the wide, double doors that led inside, and hoping that it wasn't an omen for the turmoil to come.

Cane turned off the engine and we sat in the Jeep, staring at the door for five minutes before I unclipped my seat belt. "I can wait here while you talk if you're reluctant to take me inside," I said.

Despite my belief that Cane would be better off away from me, I was surprised to find I meant it. The journey in the car had taught me how much I feared to be away from him. Though that thought had done little to ease the feeling he'd end up dead in a ditch somewhere if I stayed. I needed Cane by my side more than I cared to admit. His close proximity and strong presence gave me fleeting hope that maybe everything would be okay. But it also created new fears. Fears about how I felt when I caught his tantalizing scent, or how the slightest brush of his hand on my leg when he shifted gear sent lightning streaking along my skin straight to my core.

Cane reached out and put his hand on mine. "I am not leaving you alone," he said. "We're doing this together."

But then what? I wanted to ask. How long do you think we can run? Instead, I looked at the warehouse-style building and said, "So, are we going inside or sitting here all day?"

He didn't say anything as I opened the car door and stepped out into the late-afternoon sun.

Cane ignored the big double doors and instead opted for a side entrance. He banged on it three times and waited. After a few seconds, a man with bright, blue eyes and dark hair opened it and ushered us through. I recognized him as one of the men from Midnight Anchor. As I knew which ones were Rex and Bono, I guessed this one had to be Jameson or Lucky.

"You made good time," he said. "Didn't think you'd get here for another twenty minutes." His gaze traveled up and down my body, making me feel like a piece of meat being sized up for market.

"Yeah, I drive fast," Cane answered, not bothering to hide the low, warning tone in his words.

I wondered why I suddenly felt less safe and not more.

We walked along a windowless, narrow hallway. The walls were painted a drab gray that reminded me of Midnight Anchor. It seemed that the staff area of every bar and club I'd been in had the same cold feel. A couple of red-painted doors led off the hallway, but our guide led us through the final door and into the club area.

A giant bar, wide enough to host thirty customers, dominated one side of the room. Backlighting cast the bar in a sparkling haze of color, but the dance floor remained in a shadowy, windowless gloom.

"Where's Bono and the others?" Cane guided me to a bar stool with a protective hand on my back and scanned the club. The bar countertop was clean to the touch and smelled faintly of disinfectant, and the carpeting was newly vacuumed, as though the cleaners had recently finished their work.

"Like I said, we weren't expecting you yet. Bono popped to the market to get some supplies. Rex is upstairs, monitoring the CCTV, and Jameson's with him."

I couldn't help but notice how on edge Cane seemed. As though he was waiting for someone to step out of the shadows and jump him. I moved a little closer to him and tried to look less like a rabbit about to bolt across the road with my next breath.

"You heard from Caleb?" Cane asked.

The man, I now realized had to be Lucky, shifted on his feet and rubbed his hand over the back of his neck. "Shit. Yeah." His eyes darted to me before finding the floor again. "But hell, he don't know shit. He wasn't there when," he waved his arm in my direction and for the first time looked at my face, "well... when you were tripping and screaming in anguish."

A blush rose on my cheeks. I must have made a complete fool of myself in front of all these guys. But despite his words, I couldn't help but note a touch of accusation beneath them.

The door banged open, and I almost jumped out of my seat.

"Bono," Cane said, visibly relaxing.

"Hey, brother." Bono walked over to the bar laden with an armful of shopping bags, brimming with food. "Thea," he said.

I tried not to feel bereft when Cane removed his hand from my back and walked over to Bono before taking some of the burden from his brother.

They placed the bags down and Bono came to stand before me, giving me an appraising look. He brushed his hand over the graze on my cheek, making me wince, and lifted my finger to look at my bandage. "This needs changing," he said before pulling it off and instructing Lucky to fetch a first aid kit. While he waited, he turned my arm and looked at the bruising that had replaced the welt. "You get hit by a branch or something?"

I shook my head and glanced at Cane. "A belt." He stiffened and grabbed my free hand, clenching it tight. Bono only nodded and took the kit off Lucky when he returned. After he'd placed a new bandage on my finger and had a quick look at the bruises on my neck, he asked if I needed any painkillers. I said I was fine.

Then my stomach growled.

Bono smiled. "You hungry?"

"Starving."

Bono cleared his throat and stepped behind the bar. "You need to check in with Caleb. There's more going on than you know," he said before reaching into the bag and pulling out a pack of ham that mirrored the one, we'd found in his fridge.

Lucky flashed me a look of resentment tinged with anger at Bono's words, and I couldn't help but feel guilty about all the trouble I was causing them. They likely wished they'd never met me.

Bono pulled more and more food from his bag while Cane drifted across the room with Lucky, telling him to fetch the other two.

As soon as Lucky left, Cane pulled out his phone and turned to me. "Will you be okay with Bono for five while I call Caleb?" he asked.

I wanted to say no, but I worried he would think me clingy, so I nodded and tried to focus on Bono making a sandwich. My stomach rumbled again at the thought of some long-overdue food.

A million things ran through my mind, but mostly I focused on ignoring the fear building in my chest. Nothing felt right. Cane had left. Yeah, he had a phone call to make, but not ten minutes ago, he said he wasn't going to leave, so why did it feel like he had?

"You need a drink to go with that?" Bono said as he handed me my sandwich.

"Thank you. Diet lemonade would be great if you have any."

He flashed me a charming smile. "This is a bar. There's bound to be diet lemonade." He searched behind the counter for a moment and gathered a glass. "Ice and lemon?"

"No, thank you."

Bono popped open a bottle and poured my drink, while I tucked into the sandwich. After Bono placed my drink in front of me, I took a long sip and let out a satisfied gasp, which quickly shifted to a weary breath. "Are you able to tell me what's going on?" I asked, wondering if I should have paid more attention to Cane's plans in the car.

"Not a lot to tell really," Bono said. He nodded to Lucky, Rex, and a third man I thought had to be Jameson, who entered the bar from some stairs at the back.

My heart pounded, and I resisted running from the room. Where was Cane?

Bono must have noticed my building fear, as he leaned on the bar in front of me. "We're gonna help as best we can," he said. "You can count on that."

Lucky huffed out a breath. "Your brother's not a nice guy."

"Stepbrother," I said. "And no, he's not."

"He hurts people."

"Leave it, Lucky," Bono warned.

The venom in Lucky's words shocked me, and I wondered why he suddenly shifted his tone. He'd made me feel like a piece of meat when I'd entered a few minutes ago. I'd seen the flash of anger on his face before he left, but now he looked like he wanted to kill me himself. I worried that his words in front of Cane had all been an act. My eyes darted to the door, wondering if I would make it out. Until, as quickly as it came, the idea left me. If these guys were going to hand me over to Tony, so be it. At least then, Cane would be safe.

"I'm sorry," I said, not knowing what else to do. I stared down at my sandwich. No longer feeling hungry, I pushed it away. I frowned as his words echoed in my head and realization struck. "Did Daniel hurt someone?" I asked, fearing the answer.

"Greg's in the hospital," Lucky said. "It's touch and go if he'll make it. Cherrie's missing."

CHAPTER EIGHTEEN

Cane

I knew I would have to speak with Caleb again sooner or later. Hell, I'd need all my brothers' help to keep Thea safe. On the ride into town, I'd told her some cockamamie story about heading to Canada, but that was the furthest thing from my mind. The more I talked, the more I realized there was only one way to keep everyone safe, my brothers included. We needed to gather as many of the brothers as we could and go kill Dan-the-motherfucker and his dad. Hell, we'd be doing the world a favor.

To do that, I needed Caleb on my side.

I lifted the phone and pulled up his details while heading back out to the parking lot, but before I had the chance to hit dial, Caleb pulled up on his bike before me.

Fuck! Whichever one of my brothers had told him where I'd be was in for an ass-kicking. It seemed Caleb thought much the same about me. His fists clenched, and he barreled towards me.

I swung first. My fist connected, but he swung back and landed a cracker on my jaw that fucking stung like a sonofabitch. We traded a few more punches until Caleb stood back and wiped the blood from his nose.

"Greg's in the hospital because of you," he said and spat on the floor. "The stepbrother of your little piece of ass has taken Cherrie and is demanding a swap."

Fuck! I doubled over, trying to catch my breath and still the adrenaline coursing through my system. "How bad is Greg?" I asked after a moment.

"Really fucking bad," was all he said.

"Thea might know where he's taken Cherrie. We have to rescue her."

Caleb huffed out a breath and looked back at his bike and the town beyond. Given the location of the club on the outskirts of town, the streets were quiet, and no one had seen our brief fight. "We have to make a fucking exchange."

I growled and almost punched him again in response. Instead, I gritted my teeth. "When are you gonna get it through your thick fucking head that Thea is never going near her family again?"

"That spoilt little princess has caused enough trouble already. It's easy for her to run away from her palace and rough it up for a few months before heading back home, but we're the ones who have to fucking live with the consequences."

"For fuck's sake, Caleb. Not everyone is Amber. What? Do you think Thea has it easy at home? That she ran away to have a fucking holiday or something?"

The vein in Caleb's head twitched, and he ground his teeth. "Yeah, I heard all about how fucking bad she has it. How the longer she manages to stay away, the more fucking gifts her mom showers her with when she returns."

"Yeah, and who told you that?"

"Benton's a fucking prick who'd gut us without a moment's hesitation, but it's fucking clear his family means everything to him."

"Maybe his precious son means everything to him. His wife too, for all I know. But Thea sure as hell isn't included under that umbrella of affection." I scoffed. "Oh, and for the record, the last gift her mother gave her was the fucking tracker they used to find her and bring her home. That was five years ago." Caleb ran a hand over his close-cropped hair and eyed me as though he was mulling over my words. "Fuck," I said. "You know her stepbrother drugged her at the club. Do you really think he wouldn't do worse when he got her home?"

With that, I proceeded to tell my brother everything she had told me. The more I talked, the more he paced back and forth like a caged lion. His anger grew to mirror my own.

"Shit," he said when I'd finished. "Why didn't you tell me this sooner?"

"You never gave me the chance." I glanced back at the club, anxious to return to Thea. I'd been gone far too long already, and when I'd left, she'd flashed me a beaten down, exhausted look. "You coming inside?" I asked Caleb.

He nodded. "Like you said, Thea might know where they've taken Cherrie." He clasped me on the shoulder and walked past me into the club.

A lump formed in my throat, knowing that, at last, my blood brother was on my side. I returned to the bar with a glimmer of hope growing inside me and wished to see that same glimmer, which often appeared in Thea's eyes when she looked at me. But when Caleb opened the door, all I saw was despair and anger. Bono had Thea locked in his arms, while Lucky and Jameson looked on.

"WHAT THE FUCK IS GOING ON?" I roared, charging over. Bono let Thea go the instant he saw me, and she fell to the ground. If it were any other motherfucker, I'd have decked them.

Thea scrambled to her feet and rushed to the door. "Thea, wait," I called, chasing after her.

Growling, she turned around and looked for all the world like she was going to punch me in the face. "Did you know about Cherrie this whole time? Is that what you weren't telling me in the car?" She edged towards the door again, but I yanked her back to face me. "Do you have any idea how much time we've wasted? What Daniel could have already done?" Tears glistened in her eyes. "We've wasted so much time."

CHAPTER NINETEEN

Thea

The tears in my eyes blurred my vision, but I stared at Cane's perfect face. How could he have kept Cherrie being taken from me? And Greg... God, if Greg died it was all on me, no matter how much Cane would say otherwise. I brought Daniel to their door. I caused them to get taken and hurt when they'd only shown me kindness.

I needed to go. I had to phone Daniel and get him to release Cherrie in exchange for me. More than anything, I desperately had to get away from Cane and put whatever feelings were growing inside me away.

Nausea rose in my stomach and threatened to bring up what little I'd eaten of my sandwich.

I blinked away my tears and looked down at Cane's hand, still holding tight to my wrist. "Let go of me," I said, my voice a little higher than a guttural growl.

Cane's expression hardened. "I'm not going to do that."

"You don't even know me. I'm not worth Cherrie's suffering."

Cane lifted my head with his strong hand. "Stop. I know you. I know how much you're worried about Cherrie, and what you would sacrifice to keep her safe. I know you're one of a kind and I'm never letting you go."

The man beside him shifted on his feet and drew my attention for the first time. He was a few inches taller than Cane and stockier. His face was clean-shaven, and he had close-cropped hair like Bono's.

Noting my gaze, Cane nodded his head in the man's direction. "Thea," he said in a low and calming voice, as though talking to a spooked child. "This is my brother, Caleb."

I shook my head and tried to expel my conflicting emotions. Caleb had the same eyes as Cane. And they were both very large and muscular, but there the similarity ended. "You have to tell him to let me go," I pleaded with Caleb. "You're the only one with any sense. Call Tony and make another deal."

His deep, brown eyes, so like Cane's, flashed to his brother before settling back on me. He glanced at my cheek and neck and grumbled. "I made a mistake before, and for that I'm sorry, but it's not one I'll make again. We can get Cherrie back and make sure you're both safe."

My heart sank at his words. He was a fool. They all were. I looked at the door. Helplessness burned inside me. I didn't dare look at Bono, Lucky, or Jameson. I was too afraid of meeting more condescending gazes.

Turning back to Cane, I shook my hand in his grip and huffed out a breath. "You can let go," I said, unable to look in his eyes. "I'm not going anywhere."

My heart pounded, but I focused on keeping everything together. I sure as hell didn't plan on giving more of a show for these assholes.

Now that my attention was no longer trained on the exit, Cane released my arm. I inhaled deeply through my nose, set my shoulders, and walked calmly over to the bar stool and the remains of my sandwich. With my back to the others, I focused on taking small bites out of my food and swallowing it down. I had a feeling I'd need the energy in the time to come.

"Thea." I flinched at the touch of Cane's hand on my shoulder and shrugged it off.

"Bono," I said, turning to the other man. "I'd like another lemonade if that's okay. Then, I guess we need to talk about how we're going to get Cherrie back."

"No problem," Bono said, stepping between me and Cane. "Just give her some time," I heard him say in a low voice. I felt the tension in the bodies of the two men behind me, and closed my eyes, hoping they wouldn't tear each other to shreds.

I held my breath and waited to see what would happen.

"Cane," Caleb said unexpectedly. "We should make a call to the hospital, see how Greg is doing."

Cane responded with a snarl until Bono put a guiding hand around him and led him in the direction of the door. "Just give her five minutes to process what's happening and realize that turning herself over in exchange for Cherrie isn't a sensible option."

Rex called out, stating he would return to monitoring the CCTV to make sure we had no surprise visitors. I stayed rooted to my seat. Rex, Lucky, and Jameson all headed toward the back stairs, and I sensed Cane, Caleb, and Bono shuffle closer and closer to the corridor and outside. There was no way I could let Cherrie suffer any longer. The thought made my mouth dry and caused a strange tightness in my chest. I had to get away. Now.

Without moving my head, I scoped the area for any possible exit. This was a club for Christ's sake. There would be fire exits everywhere. My heart hammered and my head pounded as I considered my options. I needed to go, to get out of here. Before Cane came back to my side. Before I lost my nerve and changed my mind.

Finally, I spotted the exit I needed. I jumped off the stool and darted to the great double doors, barreling through them into the late afternoon sun.

Before I'd made it twenty feet, a black Lexus LS, I recognized as belonging to Daniel, pulled to a stop in front of me and slammed on its brakes. The moment I saw it, I knew I'd made a huge mistake. Daniel would never give up Cherrie if he already had what he wanted in return: Me.

Everything moved in slow motion, as though I was caught between one heartbeat and the next. Daniel opened the back door of the limousine and exited the car. Another man I recognized as Phillip, who worked for my stepdad, jumped from the driver's seat. Daniel stared at me with a knowing smile. He straightened his cuffs and squinted in the sun while Phillip darted over the bonnet of the car to reach me.

"It's lovely to see you again, Thea," Daniel said. "Thank you for making our lives easier. I do feel you've caused far too much trouble, already. Don't you agree?"

Two black SUVs pulled up behind them and ten more men jumped out. My gaze darted from the men back to Daniel. I barely heard Cane call out my name. The note of worry in his voice.

"I said, don't you agree? It seems your manners have become lax in our time apart."

"Please forgive me, Daniel. Yes, I do agree. I've caused far too much trouble and am ready to come home." I gulped in a breath to steady my nerves. "Please, would it be possible to allow Cherrie to do the same? She has family and friends who are very worried about her."

"As we've been worried about you." He tilted his head to the side as though thinking before placing a finger on his lips. "As her friends delayed our reunion, and I note, are returning you in a far worse condition than I left you in, perhaps, they can wait a while longer before their friend returns."

Phillip leveled a gun at my head. "Don't make me kill such a beautiful bitch," he said to Cane and the others, whose presence I felt a few feet behind me. "Would be a shame, don't you think?"

"You get the fuck away from her," Cane snarled.

My legs almost gave way beneath me. I'd been such a fool. Again. I really was more trouble than I was worth. Tears threatened my eyes and my insides screamed at me to run, but the only thing that mattered now was going with Daniel and getting him to release Cherrie unharmed. No matter what that meant to me.

Without risking a glance back, I kept my eyes on Daniel.

"Cherrie will be returned soon," I said loud enough for everyone to hear. "Daniel has said he will return her, and he's a man of his word." I blinked my eyes and choked back a sob. I hadn't lied, when Daniel gave his word, he would do something, he did it. I just hoped my challenging his honor in this way would bait him to give it. "Isn't that right, Daniel?"

He raised an eyebrow, but confirmed it was. "From this moment on, I give you my word that Cherrie will not be harmed." I shut my eyes tight at this response, worried what it meant he had already done to her. Daniel continued, "She will be treated well for the remainder of her stay with me and shall be returned to you in two days."

Caleb growled. "Release her now."

"I think not. We wouldn't want anyone to feel short-changed in this arrangement. A life for a life," he said, and I knew he either believed Greg was already dead or that he would succumb to his injuries. He also knew about Jacob. "A two-day inconvenience for a two-day inconvenience."

Phillip took another step towards me, and Cane told him to back the fuck off. Even though I hadn't turned to look at him, I pictured the tension flooding through his body.

"No," Phillip said. "She'll be coming with us. Something tells me she means more to you alive than she does to me."

Cane projected his voice beyond Phillip and addressed Daniel. "You telling me you're okay with this fucker shooting Thea in the head?" he said. "Seems to me, if she were dead, everything you've done would be for nothing."

Daniel smiled. "You're quite right. None of these men would kill Thea."

"But you fucking would."

"Not with a bullet to the head."

The air stirred and for the first time, I risked a glance back. Cane edged forward, his neck corded and fit to burst. Caleb placed a restraining hand on his arm.

"If she isn't in the car in the next minute, shoot her in the arm. If any of these fine gentlemen move, shoot her in the other arm." Daniel turned his attention from Phillip back to Cane. "I often find pain and fear more effective in getting what I want than the threat of death. It's amazing what people will do if you break them piece by piece. Isn't that right, Thea?"

I balled my hands into fists, my body tense, and my heart pounding and flooding my ears with its pulse. "Yes, Daniel," I said and inched towards the car, hoping I sounded braver than I felt.

"Now, gentlemen, if you'll excuse us, we have a family reunion to attend. I'm sure you understand." With that, I sat in the back of the Lexus, closing my ears and heart to everything, and everyone outside the car, lest my feelings break me.

Daniel joined me. He held my hand and pulled it over the dividing compartment separating the back seat into two parts. "I have missed you terribly," he said. "I do wish you hadn't decided to run away."

"I've missed you too, Daniel," I said by rote. "I'm sorry to have caused you so much trouble."

He trailed his fingers over my palm and wrist in soft circles. "No worries, I'm sure you'll make it up to me."

As Phillip entered the car and drove away from Cane and the club, the world around me became a hazy blur. My stomach rolled and a heavy sensation veiled my head in a pressing blackness. I took a deep breath and blinked my eyes to try and stop myself from passing out.

"Are you not well, my dear?" Daniel asked. I wanted to look back at Cane and see his perfect face one last time, but resisted, knowing I could never let Daniel see how much I cared.

"I'm just hungry. I haven't eaten much today. Thank you for asking."

He released my hand and pressed a button, lifting the small table that formed part of the dividing compartment, and then opened the compartment and pulled out two glasses and a decanter of whiskey.

"We can arrange for you to have some food when we return home. As Mother said, we wouldn't want you to lose those lovely curves. Until then, this should suffice."

I took the offered glass and sipped at its contents. "Thank you, Daniel."

He sipped at his own and glanced out the window while I stared straight ahead.

"Tell me," he said after a moment. "Who is Cane Landon and what has your relationship with him been the last two days? He does seem rather protective of you."

I tried to calm the beating of my heart and the fear that coursed through my veins. "His cabin was just a place out of the way where I stayed for a short time. After my experience with ketamine, he saw me as a child he needed to protect and keep safe."

"Are you sure there was nothing more?"

"Yes, Daniel. I didn't even know his last name until you just told it to me."

"That is good to know. Though I'd hate to think you were lying to me, Thea."

"I would never lie to you, Daniel." I took another sip of whiskey. It was smooth and sweet and slid easily down my throat. The only sound was the hypnotic light hum of the engine and the soft whirring of the tires. "Might I ask you a question, please?"

Daniel put down his glass and looked at me with questions of his own burning in his eyes. "Of course."

My hand flew to my neck and the bruises I knew rested there. "Jacob raped me. I killed him." I gulped back the lump rising in my throat and took another sip from my glass. Daniel tensed at my words and his face pinched in anger, but I swallowed my fear and continued my lie, knowing that if Daniel forced me himself, and realized I wasn't a virgin, blaming Jacob would be my only hope of avoiding a session. "Why did you let him hurt me?" I asked.

Daniel placed his glass firmly on the table and took a deep breath. "I did not." His words were clipped, and his nostrils flared. "I would have killed him myself had I known he touched you."

Tears streaked my face. Daniel reached over the divide and took the glass from me, before holding my hand tight. I wiped the tears burning my skin and tried to stop the raw panic building inside. My only option was to stay still. I'd already shown too much emotion, risked too many words.

When he spoke, his tone was pitched to be soothing. It didn't work. "I am sorry you had to endure such an ordeal. It must have been terribly harrowing. I wanted to collect you myself, but Father insisted otherwise. He made a mistake sending Jacob. He has always coveted you."

"He said that you weren't bothered about my condition."

"Ah, then I have to admit, some of the blame rests on my shoulders. I had worried those brutes would have harmed you in some way and instructed Jacob to bring you back whatever your condition. He twisted my words for his own agenda. For that, I apologize, I shall speak more clearly in the future."

"Thank you, Daniel."

"Though, I do hope you realize by running away much of the blame rests on your shoulders. Jacob would never have been sent to collect you if you'd stayed home."

"Yes, Daniel. I know. I'm sorry."

He poured more whiskey into our glasses and handed mine back to me. "Then all is forgiven on both sides, and we can put this terrible ordeal behind us." Daniel turned and looked out his window. I risked doing the same and watched the buildings disappear and the mountains close in around us. "You should know," Daniel said after a while, "I have spoken to Mother and Father and we've agreed it is best that you move in with me in the pool house. I have taken the liberty of having your possessions relocated, but fear we may be crowded. Perhaps in a few weeks when you are feeling more yourself, we can look for a place of our own."

A cold chill settled over my body and the whiskey turned harsh with the bitter taste that rose in my throat. I trembled inside, but outside, I kept my tone neutral. "Yes, Daniel," I said.

CHAPTER TWENTY

Cane

Rage roared inside me and I let out a bellow of pure agony when Thea sat in Dan's car and closed the door. With my heart pounding in my ears and my knuckles clenched tight, I surged forward only to be pulled back by some unseen force.

Without thinking, I spun around and shot out a right hook, missing my target by mere millimeters.

Caleb rallied in a heartbeat and grabbed hold of me in a giant bear-hug, easily lifting me from the ground despite my own tall stature and feral strength.

"She's alive," Caleb shouted. I struggled in his grasp. "Focus on that. Know that as long as she's alive, there's hope."

"Let me go, Caleb," I snarled.

"Damn it, Cane. Don't fucking fight me here. I know what you're going through. I know you desperately need to reach her and keep her safe. But if you charge ahead like a bull in a fucking china shop, then you're dead. He'll shoot you and then where will you be?"

I stopped struggling against Caleb's iron grip and looked into his eyes. Not for the first time, I noticed the anguish beneath their surface. To say things had been fucking tense between us lately would be an understatement. A hollowness shrouded Caleb in a world of darkness since Amber left. He'd raged for days, desperate to find her, to reach her. I understood that now. Despair raged beneath my own surface, and my chest felt as though it were caving in on itself.

I quenched the fire blazing within and looked at the fucker now standing with his gun trained on me. His face was flushed with amusement. "We'll see how fucking funny you find things next time we meet," I said as Caleb released me.

He glanced back at the ten men advancing on us and laughed. "I doubt there'll be a next time." He jumped in the driver's seat, and the car drove away. I wished for all the fucking world to see inside and see the look on Thea's face, to let her see mine and know I was coming for her, but the black tinted windows blocked my view.

The ten men advanced, looking like a bunch of fucking dandies in Armani suits, and with muscles built from steroids and not hard graft. The closest swung his arms and cracked his neck from side to side, gearing up for a fucking fight like some sort of boxer in the ring.

"You fuckers packing?" Caleb asked.

"Nah, who needs them?" said a burly blond as he cracked his knuckles.

"You do," Caleb said, his tone flat, before surging forward.

My brothers and I did the same. I dashed towards the blond fucker. Time seemed to slow. A gentle breeze carried an empty chip packet along the ground. The faint sound of traffic droned in the background, drifting on the air from nearby streets.

A brief flicker of concern flashed on Blondie's face before my fist found it with a satisfying thud.

The fucker fell to the ground and attempted to rise, but was too slow.

I kicked out, landing a gut-smashing blow.

A second later, some other fucker aimed his fist at my head.

I ducked and planted a right hook in his ribs, and a second to his head, knocking him out cold.

In the two seconds it took Blondie to stand, I noted my brothers engaged with the other dandies, and that Caleb had one pinned to the wall and seemed to be asking him questions.

Blondie jabbed hard and fast with his fist, knocking my head back with the power of the blow and drawing blood from my split lip. I wiped it away with the back of my hand and swept out with my leg.

He fucking dodged, but I followed up with a knee to his giblets.

I grabbed his head and flipped him to the ground. Then grabbed it again, full on ready to snap his fucking neck.

"Wait," Caleb said and put a restraining hand on my shoulder. "We need one of the fuckers conscious to know where they've taken Thea and Cherrie."

I scanned the area and found all my brothers safe. The rest of the dandy fuckers were unconscious on the ground, having been dealt with swiftly by my brothers. The tang of blood drifted on the air as it seeped into the asphalt and gleamed crimson in the bright sunlight.

"What the fuck happened to the guy you were questioning?"

Caleb shrugged. "I bopped him too hard."

I shook my head. "We need to call in the rest of our brothers and a clean-up crew," I said before turning to Blondie. "I guess this is your lucky fucking day."

CHAPTER TWENTY-ONE

Thea

We arrived home at around seven in the evening. The walls, gates, and surrounding forest cut us off from our nearest neighbors and made me feel more isolated than I had in Cane's cabin.

I waited in the car when it stopped in the courtyard, too numb to move.

"Thea," Daniel said and offered me his hand. I took it and he pulled me outside.

No one else greeted my arrival. He looped my arm in his and walked me to the pool house. The light was on in the kitchen of the main residence, but I resisted turning to see if anyone was inside. Not able to look at the pool house either, I focused my every thought on the pool and the paddock beyond. The water rippled in the faint breeze and the artificial garden lighting dappled its surface. The scent of chlorine and straw drifted on the air along with the sweet aromatic fragrance of petunias. A horse in the stable block on the other side of the paddock whinnied. Another part of the grounds I was forbidden to go. A horse could too easily be used as a means to escape.

"It's such a beautiful evening," Daniel said. "You couldn't have picked a better night to return to us." Daniel patted my arm as we walked, as though he were bringing me home from a stay at a mental hospital and not as a captive prisoner. "It's lovely, don't you think?"

"Yes, Daniel. Although, I'm cold."

"You'll be warmer inside." He ushered me into the pool house.

Having never been inside before, I noted the furniture for the first time. Everything was pristine and orderly. Two white leather sofas faced each other in the middle of the room with red cushions displayed on top. A match to the drapes that covered the window. A small glass circular table sat to one side with a vase of roses on top, and two chairs facing it.

Daniel waved to the door on the right. "The bedroom and bathroom can be found through there. Perhaps you would like to freshen up, have a shower and change while I tell our parents of your return and arrange an evening meal."

"That would be lovely. Thank you, Daniel."

My heart beat as though trying to escape. I wished my feet

would move as fast and follow suit, but they were stuck to the floor. I felt as though I was in the eye of a storm and a hurricane raged outside, making ready to whip me from the ground and toss me around like a ragdoll.

He paused at the door. "I took the liberty of laying out some clothes on the bed, be sure to wear them. And put your hair up."

I winced when the door clicked shut and he left me standing alone in the room. An icy dread, colder than liquid nitrogen, clamped around my heart. Daniel had left, but I remained rooted to the spot. A sobbing gasp escaped my lips and my hands rushed up to stop it. I clutched my stomach and moved to the bedroom as though in a daze. On the bed was the red lingerie Daniel had bought me for my birthday and a short black cocktail dress.

I wanted to scream and tear it to pieces, but knew that if I did anything other than what Daniel asked, he would consider all deals off and hurt Cherrie. Instead, I showered, dressed, and did my hair as instructed before returning to the living room where I found Daniel waiting.

"You look lovely," he said and lifted a glass of champagne that fizzled and popped as though just poured.

I felt almost naked before him with the low cut of the dress. Daniel smiled and handed me a drink. I took a sip before downing the entire glass, not registering the taste. He took it from me.

"Pace yourself." He touched my cheek and placed his hand on the back of my neck, using it to guide me to the table. After he pushed me down into the chair. I noted the cuffs attached to it for the first time.

My eyes darted from the chair to Daniel. "No, Daniel, please," I said.

He lifted my chin and turned my head to look at him. "You lied to me. You're a bad girl and bad girls need to be punished."

"I haven't. I promise. I would never lie to you."

"Oh, Thea. You are such a disappointment. I can still smell him on you."

CHAPTER TWENTY-TWO

Thea

I stirred. Bright light licked at the edge of my consciousness. My chest hurt and my head and wrists ached as though both were bruised. The chill from the stone floor seeped into my bones through the spattering of straw on top. It drained my energy and muddled my thoughts. From the earthy waft of manure and the distinct scent of leather, I knew I was in the stable before opening my eyes. The soft neighing of a nearby horse confirmed my suspicions.

I lay still, unwilling to move until I had a better understanding of my situation. I focused my hearing, vaguely aware of the soft murmur of voices in the distance, but no amount of focus made sense of the words they were saying.

I remembered being in the car on the way home with Daniel, but after that, all my thoughts were muddled. I remembered the clothes. The champagne. The chair.

I stiffened and stilled my breathing. Fear pulsed through me and tears sprang into my eyes. I was too afraid to open them or show any signs of being awake. If Daniel saw me, he would hurt me again. But nothing made sense. While relief that I wasn't still in the chair washed through me, it was soon replaced by another thought. Daniel had never brought me down to the stables before, but then, he'd never taken me into the pool house either.

When I finally found the nerve to crack my eyes open, the wooden room with a gated front confirmed my location. The stall was a standard twelve feet by twelve feet. Wooden panels traveled to the ceiling on three sides. The fourth contained a wide, stable gate with iron fencing above.

Feeling the bite of the cold against my bare legs, I reached out and tried to pull my skirt down, but it was too short. I willed myself to stand and forced back the bile rising in my throat while battling nausea that was churning in my stomach. On unsteady legs, I tottered towards the iron bars.

There wasn't much to see through the bars, aside from the standard tools you'd expect to find in a barn. None were within reach, but I noted my stall was one of a number lining one side of a large stable. The door at the far end stood open, allowing entry to a nighttime breeze that stirred up dust and traces of horsehair.

It had been around seven when I'd returned with Daniel and

the light had been fading, but now, a night-sky greeted my gaze.

The distant voices stopped, and the near silence unsettled me. Although I was loath to make a noise, I grasped the bars with both my hands and shook them to test their strength.

"Hello," a voice startled me, and I froze unable to answer. "Hello, Thea," it said again, and my heart soared when I realized it was Cherrie.

"Cherrie, are you okay?" I asked.

The faint rustle of hay accompanied the sound of movement from a stall to my left. "Thank fuck, you're alive. When they brought you in, I couldn't be sure."

I sucked in a breath. I was alive, by whatever miracle had saved me, this time. "Has… has Daniel hurt you?" I asked. "Did he… did he put you in the chair?" Her silence was all the answer I needed. I rested my head against the bars and clenched my eyes tightly shut.

"Is that what he did to you?" she asked after a moment.

"Yes."

I opened my eyes. Her pale hand clasped the bars of the adjoining stall before her head appeared next to it. I could only see them on the edge of my vision, and the view wasn't clear enough to get a read of her face.

"Is Greg alive?"

"He was alive the last I heard, but Lucky said it was touch

and go if he'd make it. I'm so sorry."

"He'll make it," she said, and I couldn't help but admire the certainty in her voice. "How about you? How are you holding up?"

I huffed out a laugh. "I've had better days, but worse ones too. Yourself?"

Cherrie sighed. "Same."

I pushed my head against the bars, desperate to get a better look at her. She was a tough cookie, but the strain in her voice made me believe she was hurt more than she was letting on. The brief glimpse I was able to catch showed me her skin was pale, her pink hair was flat and plastered to her head, and dark circles ringed her eyes, giving her a haunted appearance.

"Daniel has promised not to hurt you anymore," I said as my way of offering Cherrie some small hope. "You're to be released in two days. The same amount of time Cane kept me from Daniel."

At the mention of his name, my vision swam, and for the first time, I worried that he might be dead. That Tony's men had killed him.

The walls closed in around me. The dust in the air was too thick and my breath struggled within my chest. I dropped my head against the cold bars of the gate. Dizziness threatened to overtake me, and silent tears streamed down my cheeks, though

I wondered at my capacity to still cry.

"You believe him?" Cherrie asked, breaking me from my thoughts.

"He gave his word."

"What about you?" Cherrie muttered.

"Me? I'll be here until the day I die."

"Which may come sooner than you think." My mouth opened in a silent scream at the sound of Daniel's voice. He carried another glass of champagne and took a sip. Phillip walked next to him.

"You won't get away with this," Cherrie said, sounding braver than I felt.

"Really?" Daniel waved his hands in the air as if to demonstrate no-one was around. "And who's going to stop me? Your charming husband?"

"You motherfucking son of a bitch." Her voice broke on the words and my insides broke with it.

"Mind your language," Daniel said. "I gave my word not to hurt you, but Phillip is under no such oath."

My temperature spiked and a newfound boldness washed over me. "No. You promised Cherrie would not be harmed. That she would be treated well for the remainder of her stay. Every member of this household is bound by that promise."

Phillip sneered and twisted his mouth into an ugly smile.

Then he reached for a yard brush on the opposite wall and twirled it in his hands. "You think so?"

Daniel glanced at him before turning to look at me. I stood my ground, refusing to flinch under his gaze. "Thea is quite right," he said, after a moment. "A slip of the tongue and an oversight on my part, but a promise is a promise."

He threw his glass to the ground, making a shattering sound that pierced the night air. Daniel took the brush from Phillip and ran it over the bars of my stall. I flinched at the clang of wood against metal. He pulled it back and swung it at the bars in front of me. It hit with such force that it snapped in two. I recoiled and shrank to the ground, shielding my head to avoid the splinters that flew in my direction.

"I made no such promise about you, now, did I, Thea?"

Cherrie found her voice while mine had left me. "You touch her, and I'll rip your fucking throat out."

"So brave," Daniel said. "For one so vulnerable." He dropped the remains of the brush and straightened his cuffs. "Now, here's what we are going to do. Thea needs a lesson on how to properly behave." He steepled his fingers as though thinking. "I'm sure I can stretch the necessary sessions to encompass two days. Cherrie, as promised, will remain untouched. But she will remain where she is, fully able to hear every last thing that happens. When the two days are over, she'll be free to go and tell

Cane Landon exactly what I did to you."

His gaze locked onto mine on his final words. I stood and tried to appear defiant. Whatever he was going to do was going to happen. He knew about Cane and me and had finally decided I'd outlived my purpose. About time, as far as I was concerned.

"And Thea?" Cherrie asked as though the answer wasn't obvious.

He tilted his head to the side and turned to face her stall. "I've yet to decide her final fate. But rest assured, Thea's not going to be in any state to go anywhere."

I tried to stay calm at his words, but my insides pleaded for him to let me die, and my heart thundered, and my stomach churned at the possibility of what he could do to me during the length of Cherrie's stay. Afterwards… My legs threatened to buckle beneath me, but just this once, I was determined not to give him the satisfaction of seeing me crumble.

"You stay away from her, you sick fuck," Cherrie screamed, but her voice echoed with the hopelessness of our situation.

"Bring refreshments for our guest and myself," Daniel said to Phillip. "She's in for a long night, and I'd hate for her to miss anything. And bring me the chair from my pool house."

He stood on the opposite side of the fence. His face was a few inches from my own with just the bars between us. Without warning, he reached through the bars and clasped hold of my hair, pulling me forward. The side of my face pressed against the bars. Despite myself, I whimpered while Cherrie screamed at him to stop. If anything, he pulled me closer. I thought my head would explode from the pressure.

"I thought beating a woman in this manner was beneath you," I hissed out.

When Daniel spoke, his breath was a whisper on my cheek. "I treated you like a princess," he said. "Beating a lady in this manner is beneath me, but you're nothing but a dirty slut." He brushed his lips against my forehead. "You have no idea how disappointed I am in you."

He pulled my head back by my hair and slammed it against the bars. Pain lanced through my skull. My vision swam. My cheek throbbed and the metallic tang of blood tinged my lips. I fell to the ground in a stupor.

The click of a padlock preceded the sound of a gate being drawn open. Through my daze, I noted Daniel's dark shadow looming over me, then felt his boot in my stomach. I rolled in pain, but knew Daniel was holding back. The kick had been hard enough to cause untold pain, but soft enough not to cause any lasting damage, though his reasons escaped me until I remembered I had to last two days.

He grabbed a handful of my hair, pulled me to my feet, and slammed me against the wall. One hand circled my throat, pinning me motionless. My hands flew to my neck. I tried in vain to pry his fingers loose, to push him away.

I couldn't breathe. Couldn't think.

Daniel smiled, brushed the hair from my face, and stroked the grazes Jacob had left on my cheek, as well as the bruise flaming to life beneath it.

"Beg me to stop. Promise me, you'll be a good girl. Tell me how little Cane Landon means to you. Maybe, together, through pain, we can make you pure again. We can start afresh."

I tried not to whimper as he trailed his mouth along my jawline, toward my own, but I couldn't stop the sob that escaped my lips.

"I can't hear you." He licked the blood seeping from my lips.

"Please, Daniel." My voice came out a harsh rasp.

He yanked me forward by my neck, only to slam me against the wall again. "Please, what?" He pushed his whole body tight against mine and trailed one hand over my breast and down my stomach. My skin tightened and crawled.

"Please, fuck off and die."

Daniel laughed. The sound was as cold as a bucket of ice. "I'm surprised to find I like this new feisty Thea. Maybe, I'll keep you around to use as a plaything, after all. But rest assured, you will soon be begging me to stop."

CHAPTER TWENTY-THREE

Cane

It neared midnight when I stood at the edge of the tree line. The fresh breeze brought with it the distinct scent of sugar maple, fir, and petunias and cleared my thoughts. The moon hung high in the sky and cast silver streaks along the vast road before us. The road led to a fucking compound, surrounded by walls and trees and monitored by CCTV cameras.

"You think we can take out those fuckers before they shoot us?" Caleb asked, nodding to the two guards in the gatehouse.

Others circled outside the grounds. Excessive security even if the house did look like a fucking mansion from Beverly Hills. From what little information Rex gleaned from Google Maps, the place had a large main residence, what looked like a fucking pool house, as well as two barns.

"You think Thea and Cherrie are both in there?" Lucky asked.

I glanced at the trees behind us, where Jameson and Bono

ushered Blondie back to the rest of our brothers concealed in the forest. "That fucker seems to think so."

Fuck. He'd better be right. I'd been playing events over and over in my head, wishing I'd done things differently. That Thea had never gotten in that fucking car. I shook the thought from my head. There were more important things to focus on than shoulda woulda coulda.

"You got a plan yet?" Bono said on his return.

I returned my attention to the road and guards, mulling over possible ways in. Every muscle in my body tensed. What I wanted to do was run straight in and rip Dan-the-fucker's head off, but knowing that if I didn't move with a level head, I'd be dead and no use to Thea, stopped me. "How about I just drive straight up to the fucking gate?"

"What?" Caleb and Bono said at the same time.

"Take a look. We may be covered by trees here and the house surrounded by them, but between here and there is an open field." I nodded to the gibbous moon blazing like some fucking beacon and lighting up the whole sky. "No matter how quiet we are, there's no hope of sneaking up on them. Not without a distraction. Even if we did, those walls are too high for us to climb without equipment. The only way in is through those gates."

"I don't know," Bono said. "The guards don't seem that alert to me. I reckon we could do it."

"They don't," I agreed. "But why take the risk? And that still leaves the walls. If I drive straight toward the gate, their eyes are gonna be on me. That'll give you five the chance to sneak up behind them and take them out."

"It's a hell of a fucking risk." Caleb ran his hands over his head and stared at the gatehouse. "What if Thea's brother sees you coming and decides to kill her?"

"Or Cherrie?" Lucky added.

I thought about it a moment. A certainty washed over me. Dan liked to play games. He liked to watch people suffer. "He won't," I said, knowing he was more likely to torture me in front of Thea or... shit... the other way around. Just the thought of him laying one finger on her had a growl bubbling up from my chest.

"Hell, I'm game," Rex said. "Beats standing here all night."

I turned to Caleb, who shook his head. "This doesn't sound like much of a fucking plan to me."

"You've been quiet," I said to Jameson. "What do you think we should do?"

Jameson squinted at the house and nodded. "Let's go with your plan. Drive up and ask to speak with Thea's brother. We'll sneak behind the guards at the gatehouse and try to take them out. If we fail, there's a possibility they'll take you where you want to go. If we act now, the perimeter guards will be on the other side of the compound. After fifteen minutes, every other brother rides straight into the place and creates havoc."

I clapped him on the shoulder. "Fifteen minutes." Knowing Lucky to be the noisiest fucker on the planet whenever he tried to sneak, I suggested he go back and let the others know what we decided. "Set your watch. We'll see you on the other side, brother."

"Fuck yeah, you will."

Lucky headed back up the road, and Caleb stared straight into my eyes as if he was trying to read my fucking soul or some shit. After a moment, he let out a huge sigh. "All right," he said. "Let's do this shit."

I turned to follow Lucky and grab Bono's Jeep. Within five minutes, I was driving straight towards the gate and the motherfucker who had Thea. As soon as the fuckers at the gate saw me, they came outside, packing AK-47s. And their whole fucking attention was focused on me. A good thing too, as a quick glance to my left highlighted my brothers slinking across the meadow. Their goddamn leather jackets were reflecting silver in the moonlight.

My anger built as I neared the gate, but I tried to fucking push it down, and focused my attention on the guards. As Jameson predicted, the perimeter guards were out of sight on the other side of the compound. I reckoned that gave me around five minutes to get through the gate or risk them raising the alarm.

Taking a deep breath, I relaxed my muscles, pulled the Jeep to a stop and opened the window. One of the guards came over, his eyes glaring. The other hovered behind him and leveled his AK-47 at my face, ready to fire.

I rested my arm on the opened window and plastered a fake fucking smile on my face.

"How you doing, fellas?" I said, resisting calling them fuckers to their face. At least for now.

The guard puffed up his chest, trying to look big and tough, but we both knew I could crush him with one hand. "This is private property," he said. "Turn around and leave."

"I know exactly whose property it is. Do me a favor. Tell Dan, Cane Landon is here to see him."

The two guards exchanged a glance, while I tried not to react to the flicker of movement behind them. "Mr. King is not to be disturbed at this time," the talker told me.

"I think he'll want to speak with me. I'm a friend of Thea's."

At that, he took a step back and the guards exchanged a whispered conversation. It was as clear as day, neither of them wanted to be the messenger.

My nostrils flared as I wondered what that meant. It better

be because Dan-the-fuck tended to shoot the messenger and not because they wouldn't like what they found if they did. They may be lowlifes who work for a fucking drug lord and wouldn't think twice if he ordered them to kill someone, but Dan was a special kind of sick fuck, and these guys knew it.

"Out the car." Both guys pointed their guns at me and motioned me to get out.

"Easy, fellas." I pulled my arm in to open the door.

"Hey, open it from the outside."

"No problem." I reached through the open window and pulled the handle, as I did, Caleb cracked one of the fuckers over the head with his balled fist and Bono put the other in a chokehold. The guards were on the ground before they knew what hit them.

I knelt in front of the fucker turning blue in Bono's hold. "Tell me where Dan is and we won't kill you."

Bono released his hold enough for him to talk. "He'll kill me."

I smiled. "Not if I kill him first."

"P-pool house."

"Thanks." Caleb bopped him on the head, and he went out like a light.

"You and your bear paws," Bono said as he lifted the guy and chucked him in the back of the Jeep.

Caleb kissed his knuckles while Jameson shook his head as

if dealing with a bunch of fucking kids and grabbed the second guard.

Rex stayed in the guardhouse with one of the AK-47s to wait for our brothers. Bono grabbed the second, and Jameson drove the Jeep inside and out of view. As far as the perimeter guards would see, fuck all happened.

Clear night. Bright moon. Not the best time for sneaking around.

According to Blondie, at any given time, at least ten men guarded the property. Then there was Dan and his old man. They could be anywhere. A part of me wished all the brothers had ridden in and stormed the place. But I couldn't risk Dan getting away with Thea.

Most of the noise centered around the house, which was lit up like a Christmas tree.

"If Dan's in the pool house, there's a good chance Thea's there too," Caleb said as he glanced towards the back of the building.

"Unless he took her straight to her parents," I said, or worse, the fucking basement. Shit! A shiver ran through me and my neck felt as heavy as a ton of bricks, and just as solid.

"We'll find her," Caleb said. I nodded and huffed out a breath, before trying to slow my breathing.

A tree branch creaked in the wind, sending my eyes flying in that direction. I was jumpier than Thea had been back in the bar the first night I met her.

"We start at the pool house," I said, knowing by the certainty that burned in my throat, Thea would be wherever Dan was. He'd have something special planned for her first night back.

Shoulder to the wall, we edged around the main building, being careful to keep to the shadows. I hesitated. The area around the pool was open and there was little cover to be had en route from the house. A bad feeling twisted my gut and tore at my heart.

"All good?" Caleb asked beside me.

"Thea's in trouble," I said. "I fucking feel it."

"Then what the fuck are we waiting for?" he growled. "Let's move."

I took a deep breath and pulled my fears deep into my gut. They were no use to anyone out in the open.

I glanced back at Bono and Jameson and signaled them to move with a nod of my head. A creeping sense of unease worked its way under my skin. We moved wraithlike through the shadows and approached the pool house.

With every nerve itching to punch something, I peered in through the large patio windows. Fucking empty. I tried the door to be sure and edged inside when I found it open.

My brothers followed suit. Frigid white leather sofas faced each other stiffly across a marble floor. A sixty-inch plasma TV hung on the wall. The whole place reeked of Dan the slimy fucker. The only thing out of place was the vase knocked over on a round glass table.

Caleb stepped closer to examine it. "You reckon this is a sign Thea was here and put up some sort of fight?" he asked as he looked at the spilled roses on the table and ground. Water had pooled on the floor and Caleb kneeled beside it.

"Fuck." He reached out and snatched up the chair.

Blood pounded in my ears and my heart kicked into overdrive. Cuffs were attached to its arms and legs as though to bind someone in place. To bind Thea in place.

"We've got to find her. Now." Rage bubbled inside me fit to burst.

Bono cleared his throat from across the room. "Her clothes are in the bedroom," he said, and I rushed over. Sure enough, folded in a neat pile at the bottom of the bed were the jeans and oversized T-shirt she'd been wearing.

"Someone's coming this way," Jameson said.

"Good. Maybe, he's got some fucking answers." I peered out the window and my temperature spiked. It was the fucker who'd held a gun to Thea's head.

I clenched my fists, every inch of my body made ready to charge forward, but Jameson placed a hand on my chest. "He's carrying a tray of food," he said. "Along with two glasses and a bottle of champagne. Maybe we should wait and see where he goes."

He looked at me pointedly. Every piece of me wanted to make the fucker pay, but Jameson was right.

"Enough chat, brothers." Bono ushered us into the bedroom and closed the door, leaving it open a crack. "He's literally coming this way."

Realization hit me like a warm shower. If he was bringing a fucking candlelit dinner for two to Dan's pad, then the slimy fucker wouldn't be far behind, and Thea with him. The look on my brothers' faces told me they'd guessed the same thing.

We watched through the crack in the door. He entered the pool house, but didn't put the tray on the table. Instead, he put it on the chair. The one with the fucking cuffs, and lifted it.

A rumbling built inside my chest.

Caleb placed a hand on my shoulder to silence it. "Follow that fucker and we'll soon find Thea and Cherrie," he said.

Bono glanced at his watch. "You have to hope so, and soon. You have about three minutes before the shit hits the fan."

"Fuck. You two go to the main house and be ready to face whoever comes out," he said to Bono and Jameson. "We'll follow the fucker."

"Bring them back, and keep safe," Jameson said.

Caleb clapped him on the shoulder. "You, too, brother."

CHAPTER TWENTY-FOUR

Thea

Panic flooded my system. God, if I'd learned anything over the years, it was never to talk back to Daniel. He was quick to anger at the best of times. But a strange defiance settled in my chest. No matter what I did, Daniel would do whatever Daniel wanted to do. My being polite and submissive was never going to change that. Besides, maybe if I pissed him off enough, he'd slip up and kill me sooner.

I clamped my eyes shut and tried not to focus on the pain I was in. Or on Cherrie's gentle sobs. She'd long since given up on telling Daniel to stop. We both knew it was a waste of her time and energy.

Nausea churned my stomach. I was too tired, too weak, too beat up, and desperate to breathe. Above all, I was always desperate to breathe.

My nerves jumped and burned, and my body flared in agony.

Daniel's hot, panting breath invaded my senses and seared my skin. But... then there were footsteps... running. I tried to focus on the sound, but my brain couldn't think.

I opened my eyes in time to see a figure enter the stall. Daniel turned to look. My heart soared as my vision focused in time to see Cane swing a metal tray at his head. It hit with a satisfying thud and Daniel fell to the floor. Cane looked at me with wide eyes full of concern.

I crumpled to the ground, unable to take my eyes off Daniel's body. Dirt marred his suit and specks of blood stained his collar from the wound on his head. He wouldn't like that. Good.

Cane knelt beside me and looked at my face. I flinched when he touched my wounds.

"Fuck, I am so sorry," he said. "I'm so fucking sorry."

I tried to lift my arm to touch his face, but didn't have the strength to move it.

"You have nothing to be sorry for." It hurt to talk, and my voice came out raspy and hard to understand. I glanced at Daniel. "Just get me away from him."

"No fucking problem," he said before lifting me and carrying me out of the stall. I rested my head on his chest unsure if I was dreaming or dead. Not really caring either way if I was.

"Thea." Cherrie rushed to my side, looking far too old and frail. "God. If you knew what that fuck did to her." She grabbed my hand and squeezed.

"To you," I said and found the energy to wriggle, signifying to Cane that I wanted to stand. I stood in the stall doorway and pulled Cherrie in for a hug.

The rumble of bikes filled my eardrums to bursting. Cane moved to his brother's side and clasped him on the shoulder. "It's time to get them out of here."

I released Cherrie, ready to leave. A rustle sounded behind me. I swung my head. The movement caused my vision to blur, and my brain felt as though it was about to explode.

Daniel grabbed me by the arm, pulled me against him as a shield, and held something sharp and pointed to the side of my neck. "Thea's not going anywhere," he said.

A menacing roar rippled through the stable. I felt it through every nerve in my body. It reverberated along my skin and through my bones. All eyes turned to Cane.

Daniel pulled me closer, wrapped his arm around my waist, and pushed the pointed thing deeper into the side of my neck. Unable to stop myself given the pain, I cried out.

Cane stepped forward. His teeth were bared in a snarl and his eyes were teeming with rage.

"That's close enough," Daniel warned, his voice manic, and no longer the cold calm I was used to. He sniffed the side of my face and ran his tongue up my cheek. "You may have soiled her, but Thea's always been mine."

He motioned to Cherrie and the brothers. "Into the other stall," he said.

Caleb pulled Cherrie protectively behind him and moved through the gate. Bikes rumbled like thunder outside, and heckling voices shouted.

"You too," Daniel said to Cane.

Fury sparked in Cane's eyes as he stared down Daniel, but he slowly moved towards Cherrie's stall.

Daniel walked me into the corridor and told me to lock them in. I didn't move. My eyes never left Cane's face. He'd come for me and now he was going to die. They all were. Daniel would never set them free. As soon as he left the stable, he would send a few of Tony's men to gun them down.

It was all my fault.

I'd given up on caring what Daniel did to me, but I couldn't let him hurt the others. My gaze drifted to Cherrie. Not again.

I mustered every shred of strength I could, and not caring if he speared me through the throat, stomped on Daniel's foot and elbowed him in the ribs. I gasped at the sharp sting to my neck, but whatever Daniel held pulled away from me. It didn't dig deeper. Daniel's grip on me loosened. I flung myself to the dusty floor at his feet.

Cane sprang into action. He barreled toward Daniel, pinning

him to the ground. He raised his fist and pummeled it into Daniel's face just as he had Jacob's. As soon as it was clear Daniel was dead, Cane stopped and pulled me into his arms.

Cherrie ran forward and checked Daniel's pulse. "Just to be certain," she said before smiling. "Fucker's dead. Let's get out of here."

Cane lifted me into his arms again and carried me outside. I closed my eyes as we walked to the house, not wanting to see a single part of it. But from the noises I heard, it was clear our problems were far from over.

I felt the vibrations from the bikes traveling up through Cane's body and into my own and opened my eyes. We stood among over fifty bikers in the courtyard. All wore the same jacket with the skull, wings, and moon. Each was emblazoned with the words, Forever Midnight.

Rex and Bono held the same semi-automatic rifles Tony's men used. They were pointed at the house. I followed their aim and saw Tony surrounded by his men. Mom was a step behind him. There were easily twelve rifles aimed right back at the brothers.

"What we have here is a standoff," Tony said. "I suggest you give me back my daughter and leave."

"Thea's coming with us," Caleb said.

Tony ignored him. "Thea come into the house. Now. Daniel

will not be pleased to find you running away again."

Cane laughed. A nasty sound that reverberated in his chest. "Daniel's not gonna give a fuck about anything ever again."

Tony's face turned into a mask of hatred. He looked set to bark out an order to open fire when Mom stepped forward.

"Daniel's dead?" she asked.

"He is," Cane confirmed.

"Good." She lifted the pistol in her hand and shot Tony in the head.

If I had the energy to be shocked, I was sure my mouth would have fallen open. She instructed Tony's men to lower their weapons. They did. I guessed she was tired of being just the brains behind Tony's operation, and they were her men now. They knew who was really in charge.

"Leave," she said, addressing me. "This is the last fucking mess I'm cleaning up after you."

I buried my head in Cane's chest again and closed my eyes. I'd seen the last I wanted to see of her too.

CHAPTER TWENTY-FIVE

Thea

I stood at the open window of the cabin and looked out over the vast mountain range that was home to Cane and Bono. And now me, I guessed. I looked to the forest where Jacob had tried to hurt me and marveled at how peaceful everything seemed. Beyond our little clearing, the lush green forest stretched in all directions. The morning sunlight danced through the canopy and dappled the leaves in rays of yellow and saffron. Birds sang, and the wind whistled through the branches, bringing with it the fresh, clean air and the earthy scent of moss and pine.

Cane was outside with an axe in hand. The muscles in his chest rippled and sent a pulse of need to my core as he chopped bare-chested. He said we were in for a bad winter, and it would be best to stock up while we could.

Cherrie bustled in the kitchen area, clearing away the

remains of the breakfast she'd made and wiping down the counters. With Greg still in the hospital but on the mend, she spent a lot of her time in Cane's cabin, fussing over me. I was glad of her company.

"You gonna stare out that window all day?" she asked and placed a tray of coffee and cookies on the table.

I walked over and picked up my cup. "I'm not staring."

"If you say so." She peered over my shoulder and out the window before humming appreciatively. "Not that I blame you. He's a fine-looking man. Though, he was cuter without a beard. It makes him look, ah, what's the word… aloof."

I tried not to react to the word, but the fact that 'aloof' was the perfect word for how Cane had acted since bringing me home caused a lump to form in my throat and a knot in my stomach.

Something had changed between us. Every time he looked at me, pain was reflected in his eyes.

Cherrie dunked a cookie in her coffee and took a bite. "What's going on between the two of you?" she asked.

"I'll be damned if I know," I said. "It's as though he's shut me out." Not that I blamed him after all the trouble I had caused. Cherrie could have been killed. Greg almost was. It was a miracle we'd all escaped alive. As it was, I'd been bedridden for the four days it took me to recover from my injuries.

"Whatever's going on, the two of you need to sort it out. I'll not have you moping around every day."

"I am not moping." I took another sip of my coffee and grabbed a cookie. "I just need something to do with my time. Can I come back to the bar to work?"

Going back to work was just what I needed. It would take my mind off of how much my life had changed and give Cane some breathing space. He'd lived alone in the middle of nowhere for most of his adult life. It couldn't be easy with me constantly underfoot.

"You can come back anytime. It's mighty crowded there at the moment with the brothers. Hell, I'm spending more time here than I am there just to get away from all their mother-hen behavior. Greg's home in a few days, and that'll soon change." She looked at her phone and downed her coffee before rinsing the mug. "Visiting time starts in an hour."

"Give Greg my love."

Cherrie nodded and let out a deep sigh. "The two of you really do need to talk things out, or you'll risk losing what you have."

I rubbed at my pounding head. "I think we may already have."

Cherrie took the mug of coffee from my hand and placed it on the table before giving me a stern look. "I've known that boy my whole life, watched him grow into a man, and I can say with certainty that he loves you with everything he's got."

My breath hitched at her words. "He—"

She raised her hand, and a small smile appeared on her face. "He's also stubborn, pig-headed, and afraid of what he's feeling. Both Landon boys are the same in that respect. You need to sort him out before he goes the same way as his brother and loses his woman. And you," she said and clasped my hand. "You're free. It's time you started living."

Cherrie left, and I returned to the window. The mountains were beautiful, the air fresh and clean. So why did my insides shrivel up at the thought of going outside?

Maybe it was time I took the first step into my new life. Maybe Cherrie was right. It was time I started living.

CHAPTER TWENTY-SIX

Cane

The bright morning sun warmed my aching muscles as I pounded away, chopping wood for the fire. I'd lived in these mountains for damn near my whole life and it felt good to be home, even if Thea was too damaged to share it with me.

I'd let her down. I promised to keep her safe and failed. Her bruises might almost be gone, but a scar remained on her throat and in her heart. She'd been hurt, and that was all on me.

I glanced towards the cabin and spotted her standing in the window, looking frail and lost. It damn near broke my heart that I couldn't take her fucking pain away.

So, I chopped. My pulse raced. I panted from the exertion. And we had damn near enough fucking wood to see us through five winters. Still, I chopped and prayed that the peace of the mountains would seep into Thea's soul and heal her.

I almost missed the creak of the back door as it opened. I

halted all movement and stared at the cabin. Thea froze on the lip of the step leading out. She was a vision in a long flowery dress that covered her skin but hugged her curves. Her hair whipped around her face, and she pulled it to the side. Even from a distance, I noted her nerves were on edge. She looked as though she would bolt inside and slam the door.

Birds sang in the trees, and insects scurried along the branches and through the undergrowth, but when Thea took that first step outside, I stood frozen in time, afraid that the slightest sound or movement would break the illusion and that she would disappear.

Her chest heaved as she took in a deep breath and walked toward me. Her eyes locked on mine.

"I miss you," she said, her voice so sexy that it took every ounce of control I had not to throw her on the ground and take her. I wanted to bury myself inside her, to feel her snug against my cock.

Fuck! What sort of man was I that I looked at her doe-eyed innocence and had those thoughts, especially knowing what she'd been through?

"You came outside," I said and tried not to let her heady scent of lavender soap overwhelm my senses.

"Cherrie said you loved me but were too stubborn, pig-headed, and afraid to admit it."

She said the words like a challenge, demanding I prove otherwise. I cleared my throat. "I may be stubborn and pig-headed, but I'm not afraid to admit that I love you. Hell, I think I've loved you since the moment we met."

"Then why have you been so distant? Why don't you want to touch me the way you did before?"

"Damn it, Thea," I almost growled in frustration. "I think of you every second of every day. I wanna fuck you so bad my cock hurts."

A smile played at the edge of her lips as she placed her hand on my bare chest. Moved closer. I wrapped my arms around her, and she reached up and ran her fingers through my beard. The softness of her full breasts pushed against my chest, and I almost growled in need.

"Are you telling me you just want to use me for my body?" She raised an eyebrow, and I knew she was teasing. "What does Cherrie call girls like that? Dolly-girls. Is that what I am?"

I brushed her hair from her face and planted kisses on her forehead, on the scar on her neck. "You are not even close to being a dolly-girl. I would die for you." Hell, I'd killed for her and would do it again. "I love you."

"So you said. I-I love you too. So, why don't you?" she said.

"What?"

"Why don't you fuck me?"

The words were like fire to my fucking need. I leaned down and pressed my lips to hers before pulling back and looking into her eyes. "Oh, I'm gonna."

She bit her lip and smiled. "Promises. Promises."

She jumped up, wrapped her legs around my body, and squealed as I whirled her around looking for the softest patch of moss I could find before lowering her to the ground. I looked into her eyes and knew my fuck-goddess had returned. More than that. Thea had. She held my gaze, and I saw my need for her reflected back at me. I saw her love and her trust.

All I wanted was to press my lips against her delightful pussy. "Don't move," I said and stripped her of her clothes. Her tits were perfect globes, and the pink of her nipples demanded attention.

I had no fucking clue how it happened as my body moved with a mind of its own, but within seconds we were both naked on the edge of the woods.

A moist sheen glistened on her silky skin. She arched into my touch as I trailed my finger down her neck, over her nipple, and stomach, and down to the top of her thigh.

CHAPTER TWENTY-SEVEN

Thea

I loved the way just the tips of his fingers could make me feel like I was coming undone. My every nerve sang with need. He kissed his way down my body and brushed his tender lips over my thighs, tickling me with his beard. It seemed an eternity since he'd last touched me in the shower, two weeks ago.

"I want you to make me squirt," I said, surprised that the words came out of my mouth.

Cane pushed open my knees. His hot breath shot electricity through clit.

"Oh, I'm gonna," he said again before lapping at my already flowing juices and plunging his tongue inside.

I moaned and arched my hips to meet his tongue, inviting him in. His fingers circled my clit and teased my entrance.

Night after night, I'd imagined the feel of his skin against mine, the thrust of his cock buried deep within me. But none of those fantasies had done him justice. He pressed his finger into me and teased my clit. I bit my lip, moaning softly, but held back my screams of pleasure. His fingers stroked me, setting fire to my core.

"You like that?" he asked.

"Yes." I moaned "I-I need to taste you."

Cane stopped, pulled back and looked at me. His pupils dilated until they seemed completely black. I lost myself in their depths. He needed to know how badly I wanted him.

"I need to suck your cock," I said and licked my lips.

Cane smiled and gave me a cheesy grin. "And I'm fucking ready to provide anything you need."

I laughed.

He turned around and positioned his mouth over my pussy and my mouth below his cock. My throat dried. From this angle, his mammoth cock was even bigger than it previously appeared. The bulbous tip glistened with pre-cum. I licked it off, savoring the taste on my lips. I grabbed his cock, pulled it closer, and licked at the head and all the way down the veiny shaft. It tightened and hardened even more than before. I teased his balls with my fingers.

Cane shuddered when I took his head into my mouth, and he thrust his hips forward, pushing his way past my lips. The taste of him was intoxicating. I closed my eyes intent on enjoying the sensation.

"Fuck, Thea. That feels so good."

I bobbed my head up and down and he thrust deeper into my mouth where I liked it. But still there was more of him.

Cane groaned. He sucked my pulsing clit into his mouth. My eyes popped open, and I gasped, drawing his cock deeper into my mouth. He teased my swollen bud before pushing inside with his tongue. Unable to stop myself, I arched up to meet him and sucked his cock hungrily. Cane thrust into me, fucking my mouth with his cock and my pussy with his tongue.

He thickened and felt fit to burst. So close. My need grew at the thought of tasting all he had to give.

"I'm so fucking close." Cane growled, withdrew, and flashed me a look of frustration. "Not yet," he said, his voice full of raw need. "Kneel."

He pulled me from the ground. A rush of nervous excitement washed over me. I kneeled. But instead of Cane standing before me and letting me suck him off, he kneeled behind me. His firm hand snaked around my stomach, the other cupped my chin and tilted my head to the side. I shuddered as he grazed bites and kisses down my neck. My knees threatened to buckle. I whimpered.

"You want my cock in you?" His whispered words tickled my ear.

"So fucking bad." I gasped, my core on fire. He teased me from behind and trailed his hand over my breast, pinching my nipples like a clamp.

I couldn't wait any longer. I spread my legs wider and pushed back. Cane pressed his palm on my back and guided me forward onto all fours. His cock pressed hard against my pussy, and he rubbed my moisture over both entrances.

I braced myself. Not sure where he was going to go. Not caring. Cane tightened his grip around my waist, growled, and thrust into me. His massive cock filled my pussy. It expanded to fit him. I screamed.

"I love it when you scream in pleasure," he said.

It didn't take long before I cried out again and dug my fingernails into the mossy carpet. Cane thrust harder, deeper and deeper, driving my ass into him.

Every part of us was in perfect sync. Every touch, every blast of his hot breath, and the musk scent of his sweat caused my senses to tingle while lightning built in my core. My body was made for him. I never thought I could be this happy. Fucking out in the open where anyone could see or hear. With Cane, I felt safe, wanted, and finally free.

"Oh, Cane… oh… oh," I panted, my breaths coming fast. "It can never get better than this."

Cane grunted. "It's gonna get better and better." His touch

drove me closer and closer toward climax. Harsh breaths heaved from my lungs. My pleasure mounted. Cane pinched my nipple, rolling it between his fingers. His other hand slid down my belly and thumbed my clit.

"Promises. P-promises." My head spun. "Fuck me, Cane." I threw my head back and screamed as the mounting pleasure exploded within me and a wave of pure ecstasy pulsed through my body. My core clenched around his hardness, demanding he fill me with his seed.

Cane panted, pounding deep inside me until I was completely spent. Then withdrew, denying himself his own release.

"Get back inside and finish," I demanded.

Cane growled, flipped me onto my back, and licked his lips. The look in his eyes and the slow smile building on his mouth sent fresh need pulsing to my core.

A cool breeze blasted along the ground, leaving my exposed flesh tingling, and making my nipples stand erect.

I pulled Cane toward me and ran the palms of my hands up his abs, over his perfect, tattooed chest. Every inch of his body was rock hard and begging to be touched. I ached to explore it. I swirled my fingertip across his nipples and traced the markings on his Forever Midnight tattoo.

Wild lust filled his eyes, and he pinned my hands to the

ground above my head. He kissed my ear, my neck, my lips. His tongue brushed wildly over mine. All the while, he tweaked my nipple, pinching it between his fingers until it reached the point of pleasurable pain. His fingers brushed against my pussy, delved inside.

"Fuck, Cane," I gasped, already feeling a second orgasm building. I could barely breathe with the heat and intensity flooding my body and didn't care. He flicked his thumb over the top of my clit and scissored his fingers. His teeth scraped at my nipple. I writhed.

"You are so fucking wet," Cane said.

I grabbed his hair and pulled his head up to look at me. "Only for you, my love." My voice trembled. "Cane, I need you inside me. Now."

"You have no fucking idea what you do to me." He smiled.

I laughed. "I think it's pretty clear what you do to me.

His hand skimmed down my side and along my hip, stroking my bare skin, while his eyes devoured my flesh. His touch was like feverish magic. He reached my knee and raised one leg in the air, resting it on his shoulder. He guided his cock to my welcoming pussy and thrust inside, impaling me on his thick shaft. I screamed with delight. My body burned as he filled me completely, deeper than I thought possible. Then he lifted the second. He was everything I hoped for and a million times more.

I'd never felt this connected to someone before. He clasped onto my legs and slammed himself into me over and over. I could barely catch my breath. I didn't know where he stopped, and I began. We were one. My climax built as he pounded me roughly, drilling me closer and closer. My core muscles spasmed. He was all that I wanted… all that I needed. The weight of his body on mine, the power of his muscles flexing beneath my touch, the feel of every thrust of his body.

"I can't hold back anymore," Cane grunted. "Come for me, Thea."

I braced myself, digging my fingers into the mossy ground. Cane thrust into me faster with rough, deep strokes, holding my feet in the air. My eyes rolled in the back of my head as a second orgasm struck, and I convulsed around his pulsating cock. Cane growled, and pumped his seed inside me, giving me everything he had, just the way I wanted.

Our eyes locked. An ebb and flow of tantalizing shudders crashed my body, and a wave of peace washed over me.

For the first time in my life, I was free. I had something that was mine, and Cane was all mine, and I loved every fucking fiber of his being.

EPILOGUE

(Three Months Later)

Cane

From the moment I first laid eyes on Thea, I knew she was special. I hadn't realized how empty my life had been without her in it.

As I hammered away on the extension my brothers and I were making to our home, I huffed out a frustrated breath and wished she were with me. Fuck, I never wanted to let her out of my sight, but she'd proven to be as headstrong and demanding in life as she was fast becoming in bed. My Thea was learning what she liked and was not afraid to ask for it, something I was more than happy to supply. Still, it had taken some convincing for me to let her return to work at Midnight Anchor, and for the first few weeks, I'd spent every night there with her.

I stood back and admired our work.

"It'll be done within the week," Bono said. "You should take Thea shopping for what she needs in the next few days."

"She's already ordered a desk and computer online. They'll be here next Friday. We'll have to look around for appliances for the kitchen though."

Bono nodded. Thea had confessed she once harbored the dream of being a doctor and Bono had set about teaching her what he knew. She'd picked things up quickly and decided that maybe she'd like to learn more about helping people with mental health issues.

Her pick-up rounded the corner and stopped in the clearing. She hopped out of the car, and I jumped down to meet her. She'd really started to come out of her shell, knowing Dan-the-fucker was dead and out of her life forever. She wore some denim shorts that hugged her ass good and tight, and a tank top that fit the way it should. Her hair billowed behind her and in the sunlight, she looked like a fucking angel come to save my soul with a bright smile plastered on her face.

I kissed her on the lips, breathing her in, and making sure she knew just how much I cared. She kissed me back. Bono jumped down from the roof and cleared his throat before excusing himself and making himself scarce.

Thea pulled back and gave him a nod goodbye. Then she turned to me biting her lip. "Cabin's coming along nicely," she said. "I'm just wondering if it's enough."

I put my arm around her and turned to face the building, my heart heavy. She was used to a fucking mansion and even with the added two-story extension for the kitchen and office she needed, I was giving her a hovel by comparison.

"Tell me what you need and I'll fucking build it," I said.

Thea laughed and traced the tattoos on my chest. Then grabbed my balls through my pants. Just like that, I'm fucking hard as nails.

"Anything?" she asked and nipped my ear.

"Anything."

She pulled her top over her head and pressed her tits against my chest. "In that case…" She kissed my lips, my nose, my neck. And pushed her hands inside my pants, grabbing my member.

"What the fuck are you doing to me woman?" I growled.

She freed my cock and pushed me to the ground before kicking off her boots, shorts, and panties and straddling me.

She gasped as she held me upright and lowered herself onto me. Her hand rested on her belly. "I love you; you know."

"I fucking love you."

"Good. Now I'm gonna fuck the father of my baby, and then were gonna talk about how we can extend upstairs to add a nursery."

My hands rushed to touch her belly. My fucking throat

burned. "You sure?"

"Positive." She beamed at me, and my whole fucking world shone bright.

Goddamn tears threatened my eyes. I never knew I could be this happy. I growled and pulled her down to me, kissing her deeply. She pulled back. A smile danced over her lips, and she clenched her pussy around me.

A ripple of pleasure traveled up my length, and with excruciating slowness, she rode me gently at first until both her body and mine demanded more.

She moaned and screamed in pleasure, and I pulled her down, wanting to feel every part of her next to me.

Our bodies collide as one. Our hearts are one. And our baby will be one of many, cause, fuck me, I can't keep my hands off of this woman. Every moment with her is my Forever Midnight.

Printed in Great Britain
by Amazon